Prints in the Sand

My Journey with Nanea

by Erin Falligant

American Girl®

Published by American Girl Publishing

17 18 19 20 21 22 23 LEO 10 9 8 7 6 5 4 3 2 1

This book is a work of fiction. Any similarity to real persons, living or dead, is coincidental and not intended by American Girl. References to real events, people, or places are used fictitiously. Other names, characters, places, and incidents are the products of imagination.

Cover image by David Roth and Juliana Kolesova
Author photo by Reverie Photography

Cataloging-in-Publication Data available from the Library of Congress

For Tera, Stacey, and Shelley—my own "Three Kittens," who have been with me every step of the way

BeForever™

The adventurous characters you'll meet in
the BeForever books will spark your curiosity
about the past, inspire you to find your voice
in the present, and excite you about your future.
You'll make friends with these girls as you share
their fun and their challenges. Like you, they are
bright and brave, imaginative and energetic,
creative and kind. Just as you are, they are
discovering what really matters: Helping others.
Being a true friend. Protecting the earth.
Standing up for what's right. Read their stories,
explore their worlds, join their adventures.
Your friendship with them will BeForever.

A Journey Begins

This book is about Nanea, but it's also about a girl like you who travels back in time to Nanea's world of 1942. You, the reader, get to decide what happens in the story. The choices you make will lead to different journeys and new discoveries.

When you reach a page in this book that asks you to make a decision, choose carefully. The decisions you make will lead to different endings. (Hint: Use a pencil to check off your choices. That way, you'll never read the same story twice.)

Want to try another ending? Go back to a choice point and find out what happens when you make different choices.

Before your journey ends, take a peek into the past, on page 174, to discover more about Nanea's time.

Nanea lives in Hawaii on the island of Oahu, so you'll see some Hawaiian words in this book. The meaning and pronunciation of these words are provided in the glossary on page 176.

Nanea's name is pronounced *nah-NAY-ah.* It means "delightful and pleasant."

1

Overseas. That's where Dad is. So if I look far enough out to sea, will I find him there?

I shade my eyes and gaze past the beach where my little brothers build their sand castle, out to the blurred line of the horizon. There, I see a glimmer of light. I imagine it's Dad's plane coming home, dipping its wing to say *aloha* to me.

Being away from Dad is so hard! I don't know how my mom and brothers can stand it. My dad is in the army, but we've *always* moved with him from base to base. That's how we came to Oahu six months ago.

Then, at the start of summer, Dad was sent to Iraq, and Mom said it was too dangerous for us to go along. *If it's so dangerous,* I wanted to ask, *why is Dad going?*

But I didn't ask. And we never talk about Iraq. We just say that Dad is "overseas," like he's on vacation somewhere. And I pretend that my mom, brothers, and I are, too. Because Hawaii just doesn't feel like home—not without Dad.

A squeal cuts through the air. It's my brother Alex. His twin, Aidan, is chasing him with a cup of water. I'm about to tell the boys to settle down when some-one else steps in—Auntie Oli, our new babysitter. She catches Aidan before he tramples over the sand castle.

At least someone's having fun here, I think as I straighten out my towel. My twin brothers usually do have fun, maybe because they always have each other. *But who do I have now that Dad's gone?*

I had my friend Kayla in California. Mom wants me to make new friends, but what good is making friends if I just have to leave them behind the *next* time we move?

Mom has been working a lot lately, so she's usually gone during the day. And Auntie Oli seems nice enough, but I barely even know her! "Be kind to Auntie Oli," Mom said as she left the house this morning. "She's done a lot to make us feel welcome. Where's your aloha spirit?"

I don't really know what that means. How can I welcome someone new into our family when I miss someone else so much? Maybe I left my "aloha spirit" in California with Kayla. Or maybe it got on the plane with Dad two weeks ago.

At least I have Nancy Drew, I remind myself, blowing the sand off the cover of my new mystery. I crack open the book and try to read, but some delicious smell drifts out of Auntie Oli's basket. I'm pretty sure it's her amazing guava bread, which she baked for our picnic dinner. Yum!

It's sure hard to concentrate with that bread so close. Plus, the sounds of the beach are distracting. Birds chirp, waves splash onto shore, kids squeal and bark. *Wait, what?*

I roll onto my hip to look for the dog. I love Nancy Drew, but I love dogs even more! I've begged Mom to get one, but she says there are enough bodies in the house to take care of without adding one more.

Just beyond a few bright beach umbrellas, I see a salt-and-pepper tail bobbing back and forth. I can't see the dog's head, but a spray of sand tells me that it's digging for something.

"Stay away from that dog!" That's what Mom would say if she were here. She thinks any dogs that run loose might be unfriendly. But that wagging tail looks pretty friendly to me.

I hop up to get a closer look.

Turn to page 4.

4

As I walk past the rainbow of umbrellas, I can see the dog better. It has scruffy fur and floppy ears. The dog wears a pretty green collar with little flowers on it. It must be a she—and she belongs to someone. Her head disappears into the hole, and when it pops back out, something dangles from her mouth.

"What did you find there, girl?" As I take a step toward her, she sticks her rump in the air. She races in a little circle. Then she stops, her body tense, waiting for me to make my move.

"Oh, so you want to play?" I call to her, laughing.

She drops whatever she's holding and barks. Then she takes off running toward the pink hotel next door. It's *really* pink, like the strawberry shave ice I get from the stand on the beach. I'm blinded for a second by all that pink, and when I look for the dog again, she's gone. But what did she leave behind for me? I stoop to pick it up. It looks like a pile of shells, but when I lift one, they all come with it. It's a necklace!

"Ooh, that looks like an old *puka* shell necklace," says a woman sitting under a candy-apple red umbrella. Her little girl is asleep in the shade.

"Really?" I say, examining the necklace.

"That's very special," the woman explains. "Puka necklaces were given to people setting off on long journeys—to ensure a safe and peaceful voyage. Are you taking a trip soon?"

Not until Dad comes home, I think.

Another shrill bark catches my ear. This one comes from the patio of the pink hotel. A black nose pokes out from beneath the ruffle of a tablecloth. The dog barks again. Is she talking to me? I have to follow her!

I glance back at my brothers, who are stacking cups of sand on top of one another to form a wobbly tower. Auntie Oli helps balance it as Alex adds a sixth cup. They'll be fine without me. I check my watch, which reads 3:22. There's plenty of time before dinner. Plenty of time to follow that dog. So with a tingle of excitement, I hurry toward the patio. The puka shells jingle in my hand. I don't want to lose them, so I slide the necklace carefully over my head. But as I pull my hair out from under the string of shells, the ground drops from beneath my feet. I feel the whoosh of an ocean breeze. And then a pink mist covers my eyes . . .

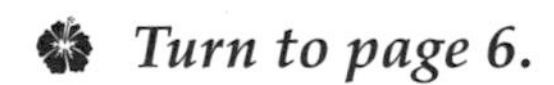
Turn to page 6.

6

I'm still standing—on wobbly legs. And that pink mist is the hotel in front of me. But now there's something else: a barbed-wire fence. It stretches along the beach as far as my eyes can see. That wasn't here before!

Running along the fence are paw prints—*dog* prints. They lead me a few feet to the right, and then they disappear. Did the dog go under the barbed wire? When I kneel beside the fence, I spot a hole. It's big enough for a girl to fit through.

Without even thinking, I duck through the hole and follow the paw prints around to the front of the hotel. But a buzz of low voices near the entrance surprises me. Glancing up, I see a crowd of soldiers and sailors. Why are they all at the beach—dressed in uniform?

Ooga! A shiny navy blue car inches slowly through the crowd. It looks like the old-time cars I've seen in parades sometimes. When the door opens, I'm surprised to see a nurse pop out. She wears a stiff white cap, and as she straightens up, I see the red cross sewn to her starched white dress.

As she hurries into the hotel and that old car rumbles away, anxiety rumbles through my stomach, too.

Something's not quite right here. *Soldiers? Nurses? Old-time cars? Why are they all here at the beach?*

Then I see a girl step out of the crowd—someone my own age, finally! She wears a bright red flower in her dark, wavy hair. She raises her hand to her mouth and calls, *"Mele!"*

I know that word—it's one that Auntie Oli taught my little brothers this summer. It means "song." But why is this girl shouting it?

Then a furry bundle of energy pops out of a patch of flowers. It's my dog! *Her dog,* I correct myself. *And her name must be Mele!*

The girl scoops up the pup and disappears back into the hotel, so I follow her. I'm three steps into the lobby before I realize, with embarrassment, that I'm still wearing my swimsuit. Do I have time to run back to the beach and grab my cover-up?

I hesitate too long. Now I've lost the girl—I can't see her in the lobby. And everyone in there looks so fancy! I can't go in wearing only a swimsuit.

So I hurry back outside, dodge a few soldiers, and race through the sand toward the beach. But suddenly, I'm not sure which way to go. I can see the hole in the fence, but nothing on the other side looks familiar!

Find the red umbrella, I tell myself. It was the brightest thing on the beach. There it is!

I dart toward it, my feet slipping in the sand. But as I round the umbrella, I know right away that this isn't the same one. Instead of a woman smiling up at me, a sailor sits cross-legged on a towel. He tips his white hat at me and grins.

I run past him, toward the water. My brothers should be easy enough to find—or hear. But one look at the shoreline tells me that *they're* gone, too!

There are hardly any children left on the beach. A few teenage boys wearing black swim trunks dart in and out of the waves. There are two women on the beach, but they're wearing old-fashioned suits with skirts attached. One has a funny rubber cap on her head.

I don't know anyone here, I realize. *I don't even know where "here" is—or when. It's like I've traveled back in time!* A shiver of excitement runs down my spine.

I take a deep breath and try to retrace my steps. I remember spotting the dog and getting up from my towel. I found the puka shell necklace and put it on, and . . . then what? It all seems like a hazy dream.

As I reach up to touch the necklace, the puka shells feel smooth, cool, and mysterious. I slide the necklace off to take a closer look. That's when the ground beneath me rolls again, like a surfboard on a rising wave . . .

Turn to page 10.

10

When I open my eyes, the ocean stretches out before me. And I see a wobbly sand castle that's about to topple over in front of two little boys—my brothers!

But as Alex places a cup of sand on the tower, I realize something. My brothers are exactly where I left them. Their sand castle tower is exactly six cups tall. Auntie Oli is still steadying it, as if she's been frozen in place for the last few minutes.

I check my watch, which reads 3:22. *Still.*

I do a slow spin on the beach, trying to sort it all out. The barbed-wire fence is gone. Children romp on the beach in swimsuits—regular, modern-day swimsuits. And there, beneath her red umbrella, is that woman—the one who asked if I would be taking a trip sometime soon.

I think I just did, I want to tell her. I glance at the puka shell necklace wrapped around my fingers. *Did this necklace send me away somewhere—maybe even back in time?*

I start walking toward my blanket, where my book waits for me. But then my feet stop. *You could stay here and read about Nancy Drew's latest adventure,* I tell myself. *Or . . . you could have one of your own.*

The thought comes to me so clearly, as if someone said it out loud. I glance at the red umbrella, which is the same red as the flower in that girl's hair—the girl who must love dogs as much as I do.

Thinking of her and her dog, Mele, I already know what I'm going to do. I grab my cover-up and pull it over my swimsuit. Then I take one last look at my brothers and carefully lower the puka shell necklace over my head.

Turn to page 12.

12

The soldiers are still standing in front of the Royal Hawaiian Hotel. That's what it's called, says the sign out front. And the hotel does look royal. It stretches toward the sky like a pink palace, higher than the tallest palm tree here on Waikiki Beach.

As I sidestep a soldier and make my way into the lobby, I notice the posters on the wall. There are lots of them, a collage of signs that say things like "Buy Your War Bonds!" and "Do Your Part to Help the War!"

War? What war? That queasy feeling in my stomach comes back.

"May I help you, miss?" asks a young man in a crisp jacket. His name tag reads "Darrell."

"Um, I'm—I'm not sure," I stammer. "Can you tell me what . . . the date is?"

"June 26," says Darrell, gesturing toward a fancy calendar on the wall.

I follow his pointed finger and let my gaze slide upward to the year at the top of the calendar.

1942.

My knees wobble.

Darrell reaches for my arm to steady me. "Are your parents here, miss?" he asks, worry creeping into his voice. "Are you looking for them?"

I shake my head and try to pull myself together. "I'm looking for . . . a girl."

"Ah," he says with an easy smile, "the Honolulu Helpers meeting. Follow me, please."

As he leads me through the lobby, I try not to stare. Sparkling chandeliers hang overhead, and along each wall, fancy chairs are piled high with plump pink pillows.

Then I see her: the wavy-haired girl with the dog. Except she's no longer holding the dog. She's standing by an open door, talking with another girl. There's a sign on the door that reads, "Welcome, Honolulu Helpers."

Darrell waves his arm toward the door as if he were rolling out a red carpet for me. And as I step toward it, something wafts out: the smell of cookies. My stomach rumbles.

Darrell catches the scent, too, and inhales deeply. "Makes me wish *I* were a member of the club," he jokes before hurrying back across the lobby.

The dark-haired girl laughs and then waves to me. "Hi, I'm Nanea Mitchell. Are you here for the Honolulu

Helpers meeting? There's a cookie giveaway for the soldiers!" She's looking right at me for the first time. All of a sudden, this dreamlike "adventure" feels pretty real.

"Honolulu Helpers?" I ask.

"Yes!" the other girl answers. "We do things to help the war effort and to boost morale."

"To help people feel happier and more hopeful," explains Nanea. "Have you heard of us?"

I shake my head. But Nanea's club reminds me of something my friend Kayla and I started in California—the Acts of Kindness Project. We did nice things for other people, secretly so they wouldn't even know who had done it. It was so much fun!

But before I can tell Nanea about it, she notices my swimsuit cover-up. "Or are you here to watch the hula?" she asks. "I might perform in the show with my dog if I can miss part of the club meeting."

Does she think my cover-up is a hula costume? I wonder. Then a bigger question enters my mind. *Does Nanea's dog really do the hula? This I gotta see!*

The other girl adds, "You might even learn some hula moves. Nanea is a great teacher!"

Nanea blushes. "My *tutu*—my grandma—is the

teacher. But sometimes during a show, we teach the soldiers some hula. I could teach you!"

The smile freezes on my face. I'm not a very good dancer. Mom has been trying to get me to take hula lessons, but I'm afraid I'll make a fool of myself. And I sure don't want to do that in front of my new friends.

Now the Honolulu Helpers meeting is sounding even better. But if I go to the meeting, I won't get to see Nanea's dog dance! Nanea is smiling at me, waiting for my decision.

To watch hula,
turn to page 16.

To attend the meeting,
turn to page 18.

16

I'd like to watch the hula," I say. But I cross my fingers and my toes, hoping Nanea doesn't ask me to dance with her.

"Oh, good!" she says. "I'll help you find a seat. Lily, can you let your mom know that I won't be at the meeting?"

Lily looks disappointed, but she nods and ducks back into the meeting room.

"Lily's mother is helping with our cookie give-away," Nanea explains as she leads me down the long hall. "Is your mom here, too?" She glances over her shoulder, as if my mom somehow got left behind in the shuffle.

"No, just my babysitter and little brothers. They're out on the beach. My mom's working all the time, and my dad is . . . well, he moved here with us, but now he's . . . overseas." The words leak from my mouth like water from a hose. *Why'd I say all that?*

A shadow passes over Nanea's face. "My brother, David, just joined the army, too," she says. "He's not overseas yet, but he will be soon. It seems like every-one is signing up—I mean, since Pearl Harbor was bombed."

Bombed? Her words start to slide together like puzzle pieces in my mind.

When we first moved to Oahu, Mom took us to a memorial, a place where a ship was bombed and sunk during World War Two. Lots of ships were bombed by Japanese planes right here in Pearl Harbor.

Listening to Nanea, I realize something. I not only stepped back in time, I stepped back right into the middle of World War Two!

My legs feel weak as I reach up to touch my necklace. *Don't worry,* I remind myself. *You can go home anytime you want.* But I'm not ready yet. I just met Nanea! So I take a deep breath and follow her down the hall.

Turn to page 21.

"I'd like to go to the Honolulu Helpers meeting," I finally say, "but I don't have any cookies to give away!"

"That's okay," says Nanea. She gestures to the girl standing next to her. "Lily and I brought extra. Some are for the soldiers who are here at the Royal Hawaiian for R & R—rest and relaxation. And some are to bring to soldiers at Queen's Hospital."

I suddenly remember what I'm wearing. "Oh, I'm not really dressed for the meeting." I take a step back, embarrassed.

Nanea laughs. "Me neither. I thought I might be doing hula instead. But we can sit together so we don't feel so out of place. We kind of match."

"You both have shell necklaces!" Lily points out.

Nanea lifts a strand of shells around her neck. "*Tutu Kane*, my grandpa, made this for my tenth birthday this year," she tells me. "He said it was time for me to wear one—because I am growing up full of aloha." She says the last part quietly, her cheeks pink with pride.

I'm still not exactly sure what aloha means. And I hope Nanea doesn't ask me where I got my necklace. I don't think she'd believe that her dog led me to it.

"C'mon," says Lily, waving us into the room. "We don't want to miss out on all the good treats!"

"Like your mom's *mochi*?" says Nanea, grinning. "Lily's mom makes the best Japanese rice cakes. She's helping us with the cookie giveaway."

Nanea points to the pretty dark-haired woman at the front of the room. I'm surprised to see a nurse standing beside her. It's the one who got out of that old car in front of the hotel!

"Why is a nurse here?" I whisper as I scoot into a chair beside Nanea.

"She's not a nurse," Nanea explains. "She's from the Red Cross. She's going to show us how to roll bandages."

Bandages? I get that uneasy feeling all over again. War posters in the hotel. Someone from the Red Cross at this girls' club meeting. And now bandages!

Lily sees my face. "I don't like to think about bandages either," she whispers.

Nanea sighs. "But we *have* to think about it! There are still lots of wounded soldiers right here on Oahu, after the bombing at Pearl Harbor."

Pearl Harbor? I learned about the bombing at Pearl

Harbor. It happened during World War Two, in the 1940s.

Then I remember the date on that calendar in the lobby. 1942.

Now I know it's true. *I really did just travel back in time. Right into World War Two.*

My ears start to ring and I can't hear a thing. I can barely breathe.

Turn to page 23.

Will you have to leave the island?" Nanea asks. "My friend Donna and her mom had to go back to San Francisco because they're not from here. Papa says it's so that there aren't as many people on the island to feed and protect. But with David gone, too, it seems like *everyone* is leaving."

I nod. "I probably will leave, too." *Once Dad gets home,* I think to myself.

Nanea sighs. "But where will you go? Where are you from?"

I shrug—I never know how to answer that question. "I'm not really *from* anywhere," I say. "We lived in California last. But we've moved around a lot."

"Really?" says Nanea, stopping to turn around. "I've only ever lived in one place—right here on Oahu. I can't imagine living somewhere else. I don't think I would want to! The island feels different now with the war, but it's still home." She smiles, as if just saying the word *home* makes her happy.

A-roo! A bark at the end of the hall makes us both jump. There's Nanea's dog, struggling to get out of a teenage girl's arms. The dog finally breaks free and races down the hall toward us.

"Mele! Hush," says Nanea. "You have to be on your best behavior here at the hotel, or they won't let you come back again." She crouches low to greet the dog.

When Mele trots over and licks my hand, my heart melts like ice cream.

"Hurry up and get changed, Nanea," says the teenage girl. "Don't keep Tutu waiting!"

As the teenager turns away, Nanea shoots me an annoyed look. "That's my sister, Mary Lou," she says. "Usually we're waiting for *her* to finish fixing her hair or something." She grins and pretends to fluff her hair with her fingers.

Then she picks up Mele. "Let's go. We don't want to keep Mary Lou—or the audience—waiting!"

Turn to page 27.

I scrunch my eyes shut. When I open them, I stare straight ahead, trying to focus on Lily's mom.

Don't freak out, I tell myself. I grab my shell necklace. *You can go home anytime you want—if it gets too scary.*

"Are you okay?" Nanea asks sweetly. "Do you need a glass of water?"

I shake my head and take a slow, steady breath. "I'm all right, thanks."

She must not believe me, because she leans a little closer. "All this war stuff scares me, too," she admits in a whisper. "Especially since my brother, David, joined the army. I miss him so much! And I worry about him *all* the time. But it makes me feel better to have something to do—a way to help out."

I feel like she just shared a secret, so I share something, too. "My dad is overseas," I tell her. "I miss him so much I can hardly stand it."

She nods slowly and gives me a sad smile.

"May I have your attention, girls?" says Lily's mom, clapping her hands. "I know you're excited about the cookie giveaway, but first I'd like to introduce you to someone who will be helping us with another project today. This is Mrs. Carroll, from the Red Cross."

Mrs. Carroll smiles. "Thank you, Mrs. Suda. And thank you, girls, for what you're about to do. Can you guess how many bandages the Red Cross right here in Hawaii has rolled this year?"

Girls raise their hands, taking guesses. But when Mrs. Carroll tells us, I nearly fall off my chair.

"A million and a half," she says proudly. "Just in the past six months."

Nanea sucks in her breath, and Lily turns to me, wide-eyed.

"Do you think we could have done that without the help of girls like you?" asks Mrs. Carroll.

We all shake our heads. I'm trying not to think about the soldiers who need those million and a half bandages. I can tell by Lily's pale face that she's also trying not to think about it.

But Nanea dives right into bandage rolling. So I follow her lead and get busy.

We all wash our hands in a basin and then tie our hair back. Mrs. Carroll shows us how to wind up the long strips of cloth into tight little rolls. Most of the girls seem to know what to do, but some, like me, are unsure.

At first, the job seems easy. But my bandages keep rolling crooked, and I have to unwind and start over.

When I see how many bandages Nanea has already rolled, I'm impressed. "You're really fast. Have you done this before?"

She grins. "My mom showed me how. She teaches first-aid classes. Does your mom help out with the Red Cross, too?"

I shake my head. "Actually, she works for the military. I'm not totally sure what she does. It's sort of secret."

Nanea's jaw drops. "Is your mom a WARD?"

"A what?" I ask.

"A WARD," she repeats. "I think it stands for Women's Air Raid . . ."

"Defense!" Lily finishes for her. "My brother Gene was just telling me about them. They're doing top-secret work for the Army to defend the island. Wow, that's an important job."

Nanea nods. "Lots of women are doing important jobs now because so many men are fighting in the war. Papa says women are even working at the shipyard as mechanics and welders!"

"I think it's good what women are doing," says Lily.

"Me, too," says Nanea. She glances over at me. "Your mom must be really brave."

I don't get the chance to tell them my mom isn't a WARD, but I think about Mom's job as I grab another strip of cloth. Usually I grumble about her work because it takes her away from me and my brothers. But for the first time, I'm starting to feel proud of what she does. Is she helping our country the way the WARDs did in Nanea's time?

As I line up the edges of white cloth, something catches my eye. A small silver ball skips across the floor. Then a little boy scampers after it. Is it one of my brothers?

I drop my bandage and jump backward.

Turn to page 29.

27

Nanea finds me a seat in the front row. It's weird to have soldiers sitting on either side of me! But if I pretend one of them is Dad, I feel better.

When the curtains open, an older woman steps to the microphone. She has silver hair, like Auntie Oli's, and her eyes crinkle into a smile as she introduces the first act. Little girls pad onstage in bare feet and bright hula skirts. They must be only five or six, like my brothers.

The woman begins tapping out a rhythm on a handheld drum, which looks like a hollowed-out squash or gourd. Then ukulele music fills the room, and the little girls begin to dance. They raise their arms and step side to side. One of them steps the wrong way and bumps into the others. I try not to laugh, but they're so cute!

The next act is so beautiful that I can't look away. I recognize Mary Lou, Nanea's sister, in the row of teen dancers. She steps gently and sways her arms gracefully. I feel like she's telling me a story with her hands. I don't know the language, but I sure want to.

When the woman introduces the next act, I scoot to the edge of my seat. There's Nanea! She steps to the middle of the stage wearing a ti-leaf skirt, a flower *lei*, and more flowers in her hair. She shoots me a secret smile. Then she looks over her shoulder, waiting.

As the drums and ukulele music begin, Mele prances onstage, too. In her doggie hula skirt, she's the star of the show—and she knows it! When she gets up on her hind legs and dances beside Nanea, the soldiers around me go wild. By the time the music ends, I'm laughing and cheering, too. *How did Nanea teach Mele to do that?*

Then Mary Lou and a couple of the other teenagers come back onstage, and Nanea says the words I've been dreading. "Would anyone like to learn the *kaholo*?"

When she looks at me, my palms start to sweat. *Please don't make me dance.* I stare at my feet.

Luckily, the soldier beside me raises his hand. He climbs onto the stage and tries to follow along as the hula dancers teach the step. He's clumsy, like I would be. But as the audience laughs, I'm so glad they're laughing at *him* and not me!

Turn to page 31.

ommy!" Lily scolds the boy, who I quickly see is *not* Alex or Aidan.

"You're supposed to be rolling up the tinfoil scraps, not playing with them," says Lily. "Mom might get mad."

When the boy makes a face at her, I know exactly who he is. "Is that your little brother?" I ask.

She rolls her eyes. "How'd you know?"

"I have two of them. Twins."

"Oh, double trouble!" says Nanea. "But I think you're both lucky. I'm the youngest in my family. That makes me the baby." She wrinkles her nose.

"I don't know. Having a *big* brother sounds pretty good to me," I say.

When a shadow passes over Nanea's face, I remember that her brother is in the service now. I hope I didn't make her sad by bringing him up. "I just mean that sometimes my little brothers are a lot of work," I add quickly.

Lily nods—she knows what I mean.

"What's Tommy doing with the tinfoil?" I ask, watching him wrap a square of foil around his ball.

"That's foil from gum wrappers," Nanea explains.

"We collect it to donate to the war—they melt it down in factories to make bullets."

"It's also a good way to keep Tommy out of trouble," adds Lily. "He says he's going to make the biggest ball in the whole world." She shakes her head.

That cracks me up. It sounds just like something Aidan would say!

When Tommy flicks the ball again and loses it, I sneak away from the table to help him find it. "Is this yours?" I ask, pulling out the ball from behind a cardboard box.

His eyes light up. "Thanks!"

"That's a pretty big ball," I say. "I bet you've been working really hard on that."

He puffs out his chest. "I'm helping with the war."

"You are," I say. "You're doing a very good job."

Turn to page 32.

After the show, I'm afraid Nanea is going to be mad that I didn't dance. But she's not—she gives me a sunny smile. "Did you like it?" she asks.

"You and Mele were *amazing*!" I say. "How did you teach her to do that?"

"We practiced a *lot*. I tried to teach her the way Tutu taught me. You should meet my tutu!" Nanea squeezes my hand and leads me backstage, where the silver-haired woman is busy helping a young dancer out of her costume.

Nanea whirls around. "Oh, I just had the best idea. You should come to my house for dinner. Tutu and *Tutu Kane,* my grandpa, will be there. Maybe you can spend the night!"

When I say yes, Nanea offers to go with me to ask my babysitter. "No!" I say quickly. "I mean, it'll be faster if I just run out and do it." So I run-walk back down the hall toward the lobby. But instead of going outside, I duck around a corner to catch my breath.

I just made my first friend here on Oahu, I think as I hurry back toward Nanea. *Mom would be happy.*

Turn to page 35.

32

When we're finally done rolling bandages, I'm proud of the pile I made. It's not as big as Lily's or Nanea's, but it's still pretty big. *It'll help a lot of soldiers,* I think.

I've worked up an appetite, too. When Mrs. Suda says it's time for a snack, my stomach growls a huge *hurrah!*

Next to the wrapped items the girls brought for the cookie giveaway, there are a few plates of unwrapped treats. Nanea tells me what they are: Portuguese *malasadas,* which look like doughnuts without the holes; Chinese crack seed, which Nanea tells me is dried fruit preserved with spices; and Hawaiian guava bread!

"I love that," I say, helping myself to a slice.

"Here, try a mochi, too," says Lily.

I'm kind of nervous about trying new foods, but Mom says I should be more open. So when Lily hands me the smooth, round cake, I take it.

Nanea called these "Japanese rice cakes." *I like rice, and I like cake,* I remind myself. *Here goes.* As I take my first small bite, my teeth sink into the sweet, sticky filling. It feels like biting into a marshmallow. With my second bite, I know for sure. "I like it!"

Nanea nods. "Of course you do!" she says, reaching for one, too.

I'm on my second mochi when Nanea says it's time to talk about the next Honolulu Helpers service project. "Any ideas?" she asks.

A girl sitting at our table licks her fingers and waves her hand in the air. Her name tag reads "Judy." "How about babysitting kids while their moms take first-aid classes?" she says. "Like we did before, when Nanea's mom taught first aid."

Nanea nods. "My mom is teaching another class tomorrow. And some girls didn't get the chance to help out last time."

I wonder if by "some girls," she means me. Nanea is so nice!

Another girl raises her hand and suggests a book drive. "We could collect books and magazines for injured soldiers," she says in a quiet voice. "We could go door-to-door and ask people to donate."

"That sounds like the bottle drive," Lily whispers to Nanea. "The one we did for the Red Cross."

Nanea shrugs. "Audrey doesn't know that. She's new to our club. Besides, I'm sure the hospital could use some books and magazines!"

Lily looks doubtful. "What do you think we should do?" she asks me.

"But I'm not a part of your club."

"You could still help us!" says Nanea, her eyes bright. "I mean, I hope you can. Which sounds like more fun?"

I think about the two choices. I do love books—my Nancy Drew mystery is still waiting for me back on my beach towel! But I've never done a book drive before. It might be hard to knock on strangers' doors, asking for donations.

I have *lots* of experience babysitting. But I know that can be a lot of work, too.

Mrs. Suda suggests we close our eyes and raise our hands to vote on a project. So I quickly pick one.

To vote for babysitting, turn to page 37.

To vote for the book drive, turn to page 38.

I help Nanea, Mary Lou, and their grandmother carry small drums off the stage, along with baskets filled with costumes. We bring it all out to the front of the hotel, where Nanea's grandfather is waiting.

I try not to stare at her grandfather's car, which looks so old-fashioned. *Will it even run?* I wonder. *And will we all fit inside?*

We do—along with two other hula students! I scoot up alongside Nanea to make room for them. "Sorry," I say, trying not to squish her and Mele, who is sitting on Nanea's lap.

Mele licks my hand as if to say, "No worries."

"Don't be shy!" Nanea says with a laugh. "We have to ride in the same car to save gas—you know, because of rationing."

"And to save wear on the tires," adds Nanea's grandfather. "We must save rubber for the war effort."

Luckily, none of the dancers lives too far away. As soon as we drop them off, I slide over to give Nanea more room. When we get to her house, I hop out, and Mele bounds out of the car right after me.

As we begin unloading the hula equipment, Nanea slides a woven tote bag over one shoulder and then reaches for a cloth sack.

"I can carry that," I say, offering to take the cloth bag. "It looks heavy!"

"It *is* heavy. It's my gas mask," she explains. "I sewed a sack for it. Where's yours?"

When she sees the confused look on my face, she says, "Oh, no. Did you leave it at the beach with your babysitter?"

"You can borrow David's," says Mary Lou. "He has an army-issued one, now that he's joined the service."

I see that dark cloud pass over Nanea's face again at the mention of her brother's name.

"I hope he never needs to use it," she says quietly. "Oh, I miss him so much already!"

I give her a sad smile. I know just how she feels about her brother. I feel the same way about Dad. But suddenly I have a new worry. *Am I going to need a gas mask while I'm here? Yikes!*

Turn to page 43.

I vote for babysitting, because spending time with Tommy kind of made me miss my brothers. Then Mrs. Suda tells us that babysitting won by a single vote. That means my vote was the tiebreaker!

Nanea is excited, too. "We need to make a plan for babysitting. The first time, it was a *disaster*—at the start of the class, anyway."

"It sure was," says Lily, remembering. "Maybe you two can stay at my house tonight! Then we'd have time to plan. Should I ask my mom?"

Nanea nods. "I'll ask mine, too. How about you?" She turns to me.

"Um . . . I'll ask my babysitter."

I'm already in the hotel lobby before I even think about what just happened. *Did I just agree to spend the night with a girl who is living during World War Two?* I had so much fun with her this afternoon, I kind of forgot where I was—and when!

But standing there in that pink lobby, I know what I want to do. I want to stay. At least for a while.

Turn to page 40.

When we open our eyes, Mrs. Suda tells us the winning project—a book drive. Yay! That's the one I voted for.

But when she suggests we start tomorrow morning, I wonder if I can help with the project. *Is there a way to stay here with Nanea tonight?*

I'm nervous about being away from my family that long. Then I remember that they don't know I'm gone.

It's as if Lily reads my mind. "I just had an idea," she says. "Do you two want to stay at my house tonight? Then we can start the book drive right away in the morning!"

"Yes!" says Nanea. "I mean, I'll have to ask my mom. I'm supposed to garden in the morning, and I have hula lessons on Saturdays. But I think Mom will say yes. This is for a good cause."

Lily giggles. "I should probably ask my mom, too." She jumps up and runs to find Mrs. Suda.

"Can you stay?" asks Nanea, turning to me.

"Yes!" The word pops right out of my mouth, so I guess I've made up my mind.

I tell Nanea that I'll go ask my babysitter, but instead, I duck into the plush pink lobby of the hotel.

I don't have to ask, because I know my family won't miss me. And I'll go back to them soon. Just not yet.

Turn to page 46.

After dinner with Lily's family, Nanea and I follow her into her room to think up fun things to do with the kids tomorrow. But then Mrs. Suda says it's time for the blackout. The *what*?

Lily pulls heavy curtains across her window, and Tommy zooms into the room and flips off the light switch. He turns off the one in the hall, too. When I ask him why, he says, "So the planes don't see our lights from the sky. They might bomb us!"

I laugh nervously, thinking he's kidding. But then I see the look on Lily's face.

"I try not to think about it," Lily says. "But it could happen."

Planes? Bombs? I suddenly wish I were home.

Nanea seems really brave about the blackout. "We could keep working in your dad's den since those windows are completely blacked out," she suggests.

Lily nods, and we follow her into the den. I can barely even find the windows. Unlike Lily's room, where there are dark curtains blocking the light, these windows have been *painted* black! There's no way any light can be seen from outside. That must be why Lily's dad can light a small lantern.

Mrs. Suda brings in some knitting with her. Lily's older brother, Gene, has a magazine. And Tommy scoots in and flops down on the floor with a deck of cards. "Do you want to play Eights?" he asks me.

"Um . . . sure," I say, sitting cross-legged beside him. "But I don't know how."

"You don't know how to play Eights?" He grins wide. He must be happy that he gets to teach me. Or maybe he thinks he'll win for sure.

Either way, playing cards with Tommy helps me feel less scared. It's almost like being at home with my brothers.

It turns out that Eights is like the card game Crazy Eights. We each start with eight cards. When I fan out my cards, I see that they all have airplanes on them.

"Do you like planes?" I ask Tommy.

He nods. He shows me his six of clubs. "This one is a Japanese torpedo bomber."

My stomach twists. "How do you know that?" I ask him. Then I see the labels on the cards. They're *all* Japanese planes. "Did you memorize them?"

"Sure," he says, puffing out his chest.

"He learned them at school," explains Lily. "His

teacher showed the kids models of Japanese airplanes. If they ever see one in the sky, they'll recognize it."

"And I'd shoot it down!" says Tommy, pretending to aim a gun at the sky. "Pow, pow, pow!"

"No, you wouldn't, sweetie," Mrs. Suda says quickly. "But you would tell someone, right?"

He nods. "It's your turn," he tells me. "Are you gonna go?"

It takes me a while to set down my card. I can't believe little kids like Tommy have to worry about things like torpedo bombers!

Turn to page 49.

I don't meet Nanea's dad at dinner, because Nanea says he's working an extra shift at the shipyard. But I meet Mrs. Mitchell, who has the same dark, wavy hair as Nanea. And she makes delicious pineapple upside-down cake.

After we eat, Nanea and I help her mother clean up. I'm drying the last plate when sweet music drifts into the kitchen.

"That's Tutu Kane," Nanea tells me. "He's playing David's ukulele!"

She leads me into the living room where her grandfather is sitting on the sofa playing. Tutu sits on one side of him, and Mary Lou sits on the other.

He glances up and gives us a warm smile. "Nanea, will you dance for us?" He begins to strum a lively new tune.

As Nanea takes her first steps across the floor, I step backward, hoping she won't ask *me* to dance, too!

"Sit here, *keiki*," Tutu says to me, using the word for "child" that Auntie Oli uses with my brothers. "Nanea, what story are you telling us?"

"Story?" I ask.

"Yes," says Tutu. "Hula is how we tell stories, like

the legend of Pele. Do you know Pele?"

I shake my head. "Who is Pele?"

Tutu Kane's strumming grows quieter, as if he knows that Tutu is about to tell a story. Nanea stops dancing and comes to sit on the arm of the couch next to me.

"Pele," begins Tutu, "is the goddess of fire. Her older sister, goddess of the sea, feared Pele's power. She drove Pele away from her home. Pele fled, but when she reached the volcanoes on the big island of Hawaii, she knew she was safe. She could not be touched by the waves—by her sister's fury. She danced a hula to show that she had beaten her sister."

"Like this!" says Nanea, jumping up to dance toward Mary Lou.

"No, like this!" says Mary Lou, giggling. She jumps up, too, and they dance together, telling the story of two other sisters from long ago.

Mele barks, wanting to join in the fun. "Hush, Mele!" says Mrs. Mitchell, coming in from the kitchen.

As quiet settles back over the room, Tutu puts a hand on my knee. "Hula tells other stories, too," she says. "Hula can tell the story of what is in your *heart*."

I wait for her to say more, but she doesn't. Does she want me to say something? I can't talk about what is in my heart. Missing Dad hurts too much. But being here with Nanea's family helps me to forget, at least a little.

When Tutu Kane begins another tune, Nanea's hand reaches for mine, pulling me up. I don't dance exactly, but my body sways with the music.

No one will laugh. I'm safe here, I remind myself. How funny, to feel safe with a war going on!

Turn to page 51.

An hour later, we step onto the porch of Lily's house. I'm surprised when Nanea stops and slides off her sandals. There's a small pile of shoes by the door already.

"We do it to show respect," she whispers to me. "It's a Japanese custom."

"Oh!" I quickly slip out of my flip-flops and follow her into the house.

"*Kon'nichiwa!* Hello!" says the man inside, taking a small bow. It must be Lily's father, Mr. Suda. "Did you save me any oatmeal cookies from your cookie giveaway?"

"Of course, Uncle Fudge!" Nanea slides a small wax-paper packet out of her pocket.

He holds it up to his nose, inhales, and smiles. "So delicious," he says, peeling back the paper.

"As delicious as my mochi?" teases Mrs. Suda, following us inside.

"No." Nanea shakes her head. "Nothing is as delicious as your mochi."

But Mr. Suda doesn't look so sure. He takes a big bite of cookie and winks at Nanea.

When Tommy races past us, still holding his tinfoil

ball, Mrs. Suda holds up her hand. "Careful!" She steadies the green vase on the coffee table. It's painted with delicate flowers.

Lily's living room looks a lot like mine, with a comfy couch and little-boy toys in the corner. But some things look different, like the red side table with intricate carvings and beautiful curved legs. There's a folding fan on top of it, which Lily calls a *sensu.*

"It's made of washi paper and bamboo," she says, handing it to me.

The washi paper is so beautiful! It looks handmade, with fibers running through it. I gently wave the fan back and forth, feeling a cool breeze on my face, before handing it carefully back to Lily.

Just like the living room, dinner is part Japanese and part American. When Mrs. Suda invites us to the table, I see bowls of soup, vegetables, and rice. But there's also a plate of hot dogs!

Lily's older brother, Gene, comes home from work just in time for dinner. When he lifts his bowl of rice with one hand and begins to eat with chopsticks, I panic. I tried to use chopsticks once at a Japanese restaurant, and my rice flew *everywhere.* But then

Mrs. Suda passes out forks—not just to me, but to Lily, Nanea, and Tommy, too. Phew!

"The soup is delicious," I say to Mrs. Suda after my first taste.

"Thank you, dear," she says. "It's miso soup. Have you had it before? It's made with seaweed, fish, and soybean paste."

I fight the urge to wrinkle my nose. Not one of those things sounds good to me. But somehow, when you mix it all together, it tastes delicious. So I fill my spoon and take another sip. *Mom would be proud of me,* I think, wishing she could see me now.

Turn to page 53.

I can't fall asleep at first. Nanea and Lily are snoozing on either side of me, but I'm staring at the ceiling—thinking about airplanes.

It's so quiet outside! I don't hear a single car on the road. But when I finally drift off, I dream of the roar of an enemy plane.

When morning comes, I'm still tired.

"Ready to babysit?" asks Nanea. She's bright-eyed and full of energy.

That's because she slept like a log! I think, wishing I had, too.

"We're not really ready, though," says Lily, yawning. "We never came up with a plan! The blackout got in the way."

Nanea sighs. "We'll have to play games with the kids, I guess. *Lots* of games."

"Like Simon Says," adds Lily. "We played that last time. And we can bring crayons and paper!"

I think about asking Tommy if we can borrow his playing cards. Then I remember the pictures on them. The last thing I want to think about while I babysit is Japanese bombers. I thought about them enough last night!

Lily's mom helps us put together a simple snack for the kids: crackers with butter and guava jelly. And when it's time to leave, Gene offers to drive us.

"Wait, my gas mask!" says Lily, reaching for something by the front door.

"I think I left mine on the porch," says Nanea.

I have no idea what they're talking about.

"Didn't you bring your gas mask?" Nanea's eyes widen. "Did you forget it at the hotel yesterday?"

Gene jingles his keys. "You can borrow mine. I've stopped carrying it—it's too much of a hassle."

Lily puts her hands on her hips. "Gene, you could get fined for that!"

He shakes his head. "That's just a rumor. Anyway, since we won the battle at Midway, I'm not worried about another air raid. I'll take my chances."

As soon as I see Lily's gas mask, I decide I'll take my chances, too. It looks like an elephant snout with two big bug eyes. Who would want to put her face into that?

✿ ***Turn to page 56.***

51

"Nanea, time to turn the lights out, honey," says her mother after we finish dancing.

Is it bedtime already? I wonder. *But it's so early.*

Nanea doesn't complain. "C'mon," she says to me.

I follow her through the house, watching her turn off lamps and light switches. When we get back to the living room, Tutu Kane is covering the windows with blankets. *Huh?* I feel a chill, even though it's hot and stuffy in here.

"What's going on?" I finally whisper to Nanea.

"What do you mean?" she says. "It's blackout time. Our neighborhood warden, Mr. Lopez, is *really* picky. He would give us a ticket if he saw even the tiniest speck of light in here." She sighed. "But we don't want enemy planes to see our house, right?"

It takes a second for her words to sink in. We're turning off the lights so that the house won't show up in the dark—won't show up in the sky, where enemy planes might be flying. *Right now.* My chest tightens.

Nanea sees the look on my face. "Are you scared of blackouts?" she says. "I don't like them at all, either. So I made a safe place. Want to see it?"

I nod. I don't think I can speak just yet.

She leads me to a tiny closet. I can't see anything inside, but my toes bump into a nest of pillows. "I have books in here, too," she tells me.

That makes me laugh. "But how can you read them in the dark?"

She answers me by picking up a handmade lantern. She dashes to the kitchen and comes back with a candle lit inside the lantern, casting a cozy glow on Nanea's smiling face. "My mom lights this when I want to read at night," she explains. "It makes me feel safe and less alone."

Sitting there in her closet, I *do* feel safe. And when I see the pile of Nancy Drew books at her feet, I smile wide. I feel like I just found my twin sister, even if I had to travel pretty far to meet her!

Turn to page 59.

Bright and early the next morning, we're back out on Lily's front porch. She's polishing a little red wagon.

"That's mine!" says Tommy as he steps outside.

"I know," says Lily. "May I borrow it for the book drive? I'll bring it back—I promise."

Tommy crosses his arms and sticks out his lower lip. So I crouch in front of him and say, "It's nice of you to let us borrow it, Tommy. You're helping with the war."

That does the trick. His face spreads into a slow smile, and he runs back into the house—probably to tell his mom that he's doing something important today.

"Thanks!" says Lily. "That was a close call. We really need this wagon."

When the other Honolulu Helpers show up, some of them are already carrying books. Audrey has a big bag in her arms, and a girl named Bernice wheels a wagon full of books and magazines up to the house. "My parents went through their bookshelf," she explains.

That's when I notice that the other girls are carrying something else, too—big, heavy masks. "Where should we put our gas masks?" Bernice asks Lily.

Gas masks? My stomach starts to flip-flop.

Lily points to a corner of the porch. "You can pile them there." Then she sees my face. "Oh, no. Did you forget your mask? Is it still at the hotel?"

"Don't worry," says Judy, who follows Audrey onto the porch. "My dad doesn't think we need to carry them all the time anymore, now that we won the battle at Midway. He thinks we're going to win the war, for sure!"

Lily doesn't look so sure. But she pats my arm and says, "I bet there won't be any gas-attack drills today. It'll be okay."

I hope she's right, I think. I reach up and touch the puka shells around my neck, which makes me feel better.

"Should we divide into two groups?" asks Judy. "If we split up, we can cover different blocks."

"Good idea," says Nanea.

Pretty soon, Nanea, Lily, Audrey, and I are taking turns ringing doorbells. The neighbors are really generous. Some of them even donate games, like chess sets, for the wounded soldiers.

Every time Lily's wagon fills up, we hurry back to her house to empty it. Then we go back out.

By late morning, the stacks of books on the porch are teetering—and the rest of the club members have gone home for lunch.

"We did it!" says Nanea, sinking onto the porch steps.

"Phew," says Lily, wiping the sweat off her forehead. "That was a lot of work. But look at how many books we collected. There must be a couple hundred of them."

When I look at the stacks, one of the spines near the bottom leaps out at me. I know that book. It's a Nancy Drew mystery!

Turn to page 62.

Gene drops us off in front of the high school. As we walk toward the door, I notice the long, deep hole zigzagging across the lawn. "What's that for?" I ask. "It looks like lightning struck!"

"That's a trench. It's where kids take shelter in case of another air raid," says Nanea. She makes a face, as if she doesn't like talking about air raids any more than I do. But somehow she stays calm as she walks by that trench, just like she was last night during the blackout.

Blackouts. Bomber planes. Gas masks. Air raids. There are so many reminders of war! *How does Nanea live this way?* I wonder.

The school cafeteria is right inside the front door. That's where Nanea introduces me to her mother, Mrs. Mitchell, and to the other first-aid instructor, Mrs. Lin.

"Thank you, girls, for helping us today," says Mrs. Mitchell. "You can watch the kids here in the cafeteria while we take the mothers to a classroom upstairs. We'll get started in just a few minutes."

Voices buzz as mothers and little kids fill the room. Nanea shoots me an excited glance. It's almost time!

While I'm spreading out paper and crayons on each table, a mother walks up to me with her child. "This is Annie," she says, introducing the tiny blond girl. "Where should I put her gas mask?"

She hands me something that looks like a pillowcase—except it has rabbit ears and a see-through window. It's cuter than Lily's gas mask, for sure, but what am I supposed to do with it?

"Over here," says Nanea, pointing to a pile of masks on the floor. Some of them have bug eyes and an elephant trunk, like Lily's. Others are bunny masks, like Annie's. But there are way too many of them—and I'm already tired of seeing and thinking about them.

Do kids really have to carry these everywhere? I wonder. *When do they get to have fun and forget about this terrible war?*

I decide to do my best to help them have fun today. As soon as their mothers leave to begin first-aid training, Nanea and I lead the kids in a game of Simon Says. We take turns giving commands.

"Simon says, touch your toes," I say to the kids. Most of them do. The little girl named Annie just stares at me and sucks her thumb, which is pretty cute.

"Simon says, spin in a circle!" says Nanea. Kids start twirling, laughing, and bumping into one another.

"Jump in the air!" I shout.

One boy jumps, and Lily says, "Uh-oh. She didn't say 'Simon Says!' You're out, but you get to color with me." The boy happily sits down next to Lily and reaches for a crayon.

This is working! I think. *Everyone's having fun.*

Until the shrill sound of a siren rips through the cafeteria.

Lily slaps her hands over her ears, and a couple of kids start to cry.

"What's that?" I shriek, covering my own ears.

Nanea's eyes are wide. "Air raid siren," she says. "We have to get the kids to the shelter!"

Turn to page 64.

After Nanea and I talk and read for a while, she presses her ear to the closet door, listening. "I hope Tutu and Tutu Kane didn't leave without saying good-bye," she says. "Let's go check!"

She hops up and whips open the door, letting in a wave of cool air. I take a deep breath and follow the bobbing candlelight into the living room.

"Nanea, turn out the light!" Mary Lou scolds from the couch.

Nanea blows out the candle, but not before I catch Tutu Kane winking at her. "I can still see you," he teases her.

"No you can't!" she laughs.

"I can see you right here—in my heart," says Tutu Kane.

I sure can't see Nanea. My eyes haven't gotten used to the dark. But I *feel* her when she steps backward onto my foot. "Ouch!"

"Oh, sorry," Nanea giggles.

From the other side of the room, Mrs. Mitchell says, "Oh, dear! Look at the time. Tutu and Tutu Kane are cutting it awfully close to curfew."

"Curfew?" I ask.

"No one can be on the streets after nine o'clock unless they have a special pass," says Nanea. "It's a rule since the war started. You could get arrested!"

"Really?" I say. "Even kids?"

"I think so," Nanea says. "Mom, maybe Tutu and Tutu Kane can sleep over, too!"

"I think they'll have to," says Mrs. Mitchell. "They don't have enough time to walk home."

It takes some time to figure out where everyone is going to sleep. "I feel bad that Mary Lou has to sleep in the living room," I say as I follow Nanea into her room. I can hear Tutu and Tutu Kane settling into Mary Lou's bedroom next door.

"It's okay," says Nanea. "She'll be snoring in no time—you'll see." She flicks on the light in the bedroom so I can see where the bed is, and then she quickly turns it off again. "This is David's room, but when he joined the army a few weeks ago, he said I could have it. I like being in here, but I don't want to change anything. I want it to stay just the same, as if he were still right here. I like that it smells like him—Old Spice."

I can hear the smile in her voice, but also the

sadness. So I decide to share something with her that I've never told *anyone.* "When my dad left," I say into the darkness, "I snuck one of his T-shirts out of the hamper. I wrapped it around my pillow. I sleep with it every night."

Nanea doesn't say anything at first. When she does, her voice sounds wobbly. "I like that you did that. I'll bet David has a smelly old shirt around here somewhere, too."

That makes us both laugh, which feels really good.

We don't say anything else. But I know that when it comes to missing someone, my new friend knows exactly how I feel.

Turn to page 66.

Nancy Drew!" As I slide the book out from the bottom, the whole stack wobbles. "I love these mysteries."

Nanea hops to her feet. "Really? Me, too! But why is a kid's book in that stack? These are supposed to be books for grown-ups."

Lily shrugs. "It must have gotten mixed in."

"I think I've read this one," says Nanea, reaching for the book. "Have you?"

I nod and grin. I can't believe Nanea reads Nancy Drew mysteries, too!

When she opens the cover of the book, something slips out. "Look, a photograph!"

We all gather around the picture. It's a black-and-white photo of a man holding a little girl in his arms.

"She's so cute," says Nanea. "I wonder if that little girl is the owner of this book. Maybe she's older now."

"She would want it back," says Lily.

"And she'd for sure want the picture back," I add. The man in the photo must be her father. My stomach twists, thinking about my own dad so far away. Sometimes I'm afraid I'll forget what he looks like, so I keep pictures of him all over my room.

"Look, there's a name inside." Nanea points at a signature on the first page. "Anzu Sato."

"That's a Japanese name," says Lily. "But I don't know her. Do you?"

Nanea shakes her head.

"It's a mystery," I say, studying the picture.

Then Nanea looks up at me, her eyes bright. "Should we solve it?" she asks. "Maybe we can find this girl!"

Lily smiles, too. "Let's do it!"

Another adventure, I think happily.

Turn to page 70.

I want to wait for the mothers to come and get their kids. The sound of the siren is so scary, it makes me want *my* mother!

Nanea looks scared, too. But she jumps right up and says we have to get the kids to the trench—*now*. "Grab the gas masks!" she says, pointing to the pile.

While Lily and I grab armfuls of the heavy masks, Nanea claps her hands to get the kids' attention. "Simon says, follow me!" She marches toward the door, and the kids fall in line behind her, swinging their arms and raising their knees.

She leads them right outside to a shelter dug into the ground. As Lily and I hurry out behind her, I scan the sky, looking for airplanes. "It's probably just a drill," says Lily. But she looks as nervous as I feel.

"Do we need to put on the masks?" I ask, remembering suddenly that I don't have one. I wish now that I'd borrowed Gene's!

She shakes her head. "Not unless we hear the gong of the gas alarm. That'll mean poison gas is in the air."

Poison gas? Those words make me shiver. At the trench, Nanea is helping the kids into the deep hole, one by one. Then I hand the gas masks down to her.

By the time I'm sitting in that dark, damp trench, my heart is thudding in my ears. And I really, *really* want to go home.

"Let's cover our heads," I hear Nanea say. "Like this." She and Lily show the kids how to protect their heads with their hands.

Then I hear someone crying. It's Annie. She's sitting in a corner of the shelter, not too far from me, and tears are streaming down her face.

I know just how she feels! I wish I could comfort her, but I don't think I can stand up right now. My legs feel like wet noodles.

Nanea and Lily know what to do, I think, squeezing my eyes shut. But Annie's cries grow louder.

To stay put a little longer, turn to page 71.

To comfort Annie, turn to page 80.

"Rise and shine, sleepyheads."

There's a tap on the door. I'm about to beg for another minute of sleep when I remember. I'm not at home—not even close!

Nanea and I sit up at the same time. She looks as rumpled as I feel. But when our eyes meet, she grins.

"Portuguese sausage!" she says.

I hear a bark, and a wet nose pushes into my hand. Mele! She must have been sleeping on the floor beside the bed, at least until she heard the word sausage.

"Yes, sausage and rice and eggs—for girls and dogs." Mrs. Mitchell smiles. "But Tutu and Tutu Kane have to leave soon, so don't dillydally."

A few minutes later, we're sitting around the breakfast table with Nanea's grandparents. Her dad is there, too, home after working the night shift. He smiles broadly when Nanea introduces us, and then he asks her, "How's my sunshine?"

I'm surprised to see that Mr. Mitchell has red hair and blue eyes. He doesn't look like Nanea at all! But as she wraps her arms around his neck and gives him a squeeze, I can see that they're super close. And I feel a pang in my heart for my own dad. Ouch.

The sausage isn't a link like I'm used to. It's a small round patty that's a little bit spicy. It's delicious, and I say yes when Nanea's mom offers me more.

When Tutu Kane reaches for more butter, Tutu slaps his hand gently. "Not so much," she says.

"It's okay," says Mrs. Mitchell, sliding the dish toward Tutu Kane. "You brought it, after all. It's a treat to have real butter."

"Instead of oleo-*mar*-gar-ine!" sings Mary Lou as she dances into the kitchen. "With yellow food coloring added to make it look like butter. Blech!"

Nanea giggles, but Mrs. Mitchell gives Mary Lou a stern look. "Remember, Mary Lou: We should be grateful for what we have during this war. Hawaii doesn't have as many food shortages as the mainland."

As Mary Lou slides into a chair, Mr. Mitchell winks at her. Then he helps himself to some real butter. I'm suddenly craving it, too. I never thought of butter as a special treat before, but it sure sounds better than oleomargarine!

"I, for one, am grateful for this delicious fruit. Papaya?" Mrs. Mitchell asks me. She's holding a lumpy yellow-green fruit.

My mom has been trying to get me to try new fruits, but I've been holding out. Then Nanea says, "You have to try it with fresh lemon juice."

Mrs. Mitchell cuts the fruit in half and scoops out the seeds. She gives half to Nanea and half to me, and Nanea shows me how to squeeze the juice from a lemon over the top.

Everyone watches my first bite. The fruit smells like flowers but tastes sweet. As juice dribbles down my chin, I give Nanea a thumbs-up.

"It's good to try new things," says Tutu Kane with a wink.

"Like hula," says Nanea. "You should come to lessons with me! Tutu teaches them on Saturday mornings."

The papaya sticks in my throat. Dancing in the living room with Nanea is one thing. Dancing in the daylight—in front of other students—is another!

Tutu takes a slow sip of coffee, watching me. "Maybe today, you teach your new friend here at home," she says to Nanea.

Nanea nods. "We could make up our own dance. It would be fun!"

Spending more time with Nanea *would* be fun, but I'm still scared to dance in front of her.

She must see that, because she says, "Or do you like to garden? Mele and I have been helping a neighbor—Mrs. Watson—in her Victory Garden. You could help, too!"

To agree to hula lessons, turn to page 86.

To agree to garden, turn to page 72.

Lily's brother Gene pulls up and gets out of his car. "Wow. That's quite a haul. Help me pack up the car, and I'll take them over to the hospital."

We carry stacks from the porch to the car—except for the Nancy Drew book. Nanea sets that one carefully by the front door.

When Gene's trunk and backseat are full, he says, "Hey, when I get back, do you girls want to catch the new Sherlock Holmes movie?"

"Yes!" says Lily. "But, wait . . . we might have our own mystery to solve this afternoon."

Gene raises an eyebrow. "Really? Sounds interesting. Well, think about it. I'll be back soon."

As he pulls away, Lily turns to us. "Should we go to the movie? I do like Sherlock Holmes."

"Or should we find the mysterious Anzu Sato?" Nanea asks.

To search for the owner of the book, turn to page 77.

To go to the movie, turn to page 82.

I wait too long to go to Annie. By the time I decide to stand up, Nanea's mom and the other mothers are stepping down into the trench. I'm relieved to see them. But when Annie crawls into her mother's arms and starts sobbing, I feel more ashamed than anything. Why didn't I try to help her? Instead, I cowered in the corner, just like a little kid!

When the drill is finally over, Nanea helps me out of the trench.

"I'm sorry I didn't help more," I say, afraid to look her in the eye.

"It's okay," she says. "I was scared, too. See?" She holds up her hand, and I'm surprised to see it shaking a little. Then she reaches for my hand, and we hurry back toward the school.

Mrs. Mitchell cancels the first-aid class after that. The kids are too afraid to be apart from their moms again. And that's okay with me, because right now, I just want to go home to *my* mom, too.

Turn to page 87.

Gardening sounds fun!" I say quickly. At least it sounds like more fun than dancing in front of Nanea and her family. And if her dog is coming, too, I'm in!

Before we leave, Nanea grabs her gas mask, which is hanging from a hook by the door. "Oh! I'll get David's for you," she says, disappearing into the bedroom.

David's mask isn't in a pretty flowery sack like Nanea's. It's big and ugly—with bug-like eyeholes. There's a canister hanging from the bottom that looks like an elephant's trunk. I don't want to touch the mask. I get scared just looking at it!

"Do you think we'll need to use them?" I ask, almost afraid of what she'll say.

Nanea shakes her head. "It's just in case. Because Japan used poison gas in China, remember? It's good we have them, but, boy, they sure get heavy."

She's not kidding. As we walk to Mrs. Watson's, I keep shifting the mask from one hand to the other. In front of us, Mele stops to sniff every pot, plant, and bush.

"I can't picture your dog gardening," I say, giggling.

What I *can* picture is Mele digging something up, the way she dug up the puka shell necklace on the beach.

"Mostly, she keeps me company," says Nanea. "And Mrs. Watson likes to see her, too. I think Mrs. Watson gets lonely. She doesn't have family here on Oahu. Maybe Mele feels like family to her. Is that right, silly *poi* dog?"

Mele wags her tail, as if she understands.

"What's a poi dog?" I ask, pronouncing *poi* like "boy," the way Nanea does.

I've eaten poi before. Auntie Oli made it for lunch. I watched her mash up a vegetable called a *taro* and add water until it was smooth and sticky. It reminded me of purple mashed potatoes—except sweeter. But I've never heard of a poi *dog*.

"Tutu Kane says settlers brought dogs to Hawaii a thousand years ago," says Nanea. "The dogs ate poi, so that's how they got the name. Now poi dog means a mixed breed—that's what Mele is. And she sure loves eating sausage and fish, right, Mele?"

Mele barks a firm yes, which makes me laugh.

"She knows the word *fish*." Nanea smiles. And sure enough, Mele barks again when she hears the word.

"No, silly dog. I don't have any for you. But maybe Mrs. Watson will give you a cracker."

Pretty soon, we stop in front of a house with a tidy white fence. A path of stones leads to the front door, where Mrs. Watson waits on the porch.

"Ah, Nanea," she says. "You brought a helper!" At first, I think she's talking about Mele, but she smiles at me and extends her hand. Then she pushes up her pointy glasses and adjusts the kerchief tied around her gray hair. "Well, c'mon, girls. Let's go out back."

She leads us to a huge garden. I recognize green beans and carrots, but most of the garden seems taken over by big leafy plants.

"As you can see," says Mrs. Watson, "the lima beans are flourishing. They're about the only thing surviving this drought." She waves her hand in front of her face. "I'll go fix some lemonade while you two get started."

"Lima beans. Blech," says Nanea as soon as Mrs. Watson is out of earshot. "I hope she doesn't send any home with us!"

I watch Mele curl up beneath a large tree, in a patch of cool shade. Then I see the huge green balls hanging among the pointed leaves of the tree. "Wow.

Those kind of look like lima beans—big ones!" I say, pointing.

"The mangoes?" asks Nanea. "Oh, they do!"

I can't believe a mango tree is growing right here in Mrs. Watson's backyard. "Can I eat one?" I ask, stepping closer.

"Not unless you want a stomach ache," says Nanea. "They're not ripe yet! You have to wait till they turn orangey-yellow and get softer. But you can eat one of these." She hands me a green bean, which snaps in my mouth.

"Can I help weed?" I offer.

"Sure. It's nice to have help today! Mrs. Watson has one of the biggest Victory Gardens I've seen, and she shares with her neighbors. Tutu says gardens like this help make up for the food we can't get during the war."

"Well," I say, kneeling beside her, "it doesn't look like anyone's going to run out of lima beans anytime soon!"

As I tug on a weed, a shrill, high-pitched siren suddenly goes off. It sends a shock from my fingertips to my toes.

"What is that?" I cry, covering my ears.

Nanea says something I can't hear. Then she runs toward Mele, who is whining and pacing beneath the mango tree.

"What is it?" I shout again, jumping to my feet.

This time I hear Nanea loud and clear.

"Air raid!"

Turn to page 89.

I think Anzu would want her book back," I say. What I'm really thinking is, *I'll bet she wants that picture back—especially if her dad is gone, like mine.*

"But how do we find her?" asks Lily.

"What would Nancy Drew do?" Nanea and I say at the exact same time.

"Jinx!" I say, a second before she does. Then we start giggling and can't stop. Sometimes I forget that Nanea grew up so long ago. She's so much like me!

When we finally catch our breath, Lily smiles and shakes her head. "So, girl detectives, what *would* Nancy Drew do?"

Good question. I rack my brain, trying to remember the last mystery I read. "I think she would interview witnesses. Right, Nanea?" I say her name to make sure to unjinx her.

"Right," says Nanea, nodding.

"Witnesses?" asks Lily, confused. "But there wasn't a crime!"

"No, but there was an accident," says Nanea. "An accidental book donation. One of your neighbors gave us this book. If we interview them, we'll find out who!"

We hop up off the porch steps, but Nanea freezes. "Wait, we need a notebook. We have to write down the facts."

"Good thinking," I say. This'll be fun!

Lily disappears inside the house and comes back out with a notebook and pencil. I'm disappointed that there's only one, but I'm thrilled when she hands it to me. So I quickly jot down a few facts.

Fact 1: A neighbor donated a Nancy Drew book by accident.

Fact 2: The owner of the book is named Anzu Sato.

Fact 3: Anzu Sato must be a neighbor!

"Which house do we go to first?" I ask, eager to get started.

Lily leads the way, and Nanea does the interviewing. I jot down neighbors' names as we go.

But after we've covered a full block, we don't have any new facts. The book doesn't belong to any of the neighbors on this block. And no one has heard of Anzu Sato!

Turn to page 93.

Annie sounds so scared. If that were one of my little brothers crying, I'd run to him in a second! So I force myself to stand up, even though my legs feel weak. I take short, stiff steps toward Annie, and then I sink down beside her.

"I want Mommy," says Annie, starting to hiccup.

"I know, sweetie," I say. "Do you want to sit on my lap?"

She nods and crawls onto my lap right away. She presses her face into my chest, and then says, "What's this?" She touches my necklace.

"Those are puka shells," I tell her. "Lots of them, right?" Then I have an idea—a way to help her feel less scared. "Do you want to count them?"

She nods and starts counting the shells, gently spinning the strand around my neck.

When I glance up, Nanea is smiling at me. And some of the other kids are paying attention, too. That gives me another idea. "Who can guess how many shells are on my necklace?" I ask.

"Seventeen!" says one little boy.

"A hundred million!" jokes another boy.

"This many!" says a girl, holding up all ten fingers.

They're still guessing numbers when their moms arrive. Mrs. Mitchell is the first to step down into the trench. "Good job," she says to Nanea. "You got them here very quickly."

As the other mothers step into the shelter, their kids rush toward them. It's crowded, but I can tell the kids feel better now with their moms nearby—and I do, too.

But when another siren sounds, I jump. *Is that the gas mask alarm?*

Turn to page 103.

Sherlock Holmes is kind of like Nancy Drew," I point out to Nanea and Lily. "I mean, they're both detectives."

Lily grins. "We should go to the movie."

"Okay," says Nanea. "Maybe we'll get some tips for tracking down owners of lost books." She sighs and sets the Nancy Drew book aside.

Mrs. Suda fixes us some lunch, and then we pile into the back of Gene's car. I'm still not used to the old-time cars I'm seeing everywhere.

There's lots of room in the backseat, even though Lily's and Nanea's gas masks take up most of the floor. But there aren't any seatbelts! And I'm surprised by how the front seat is like one long couch instead of two separate chairs.

As we drive downtown, we see more and more cars like Gene's in dark colors: deep blues, blacks, and browns. But every once in a while, I see something familiar: Jeeps! Most of them are army green. My dad drives an old Jeep when he's home. Now, though, it just sits in the driveway, waiting for him.

There's a mass of people outside the theater when Gene pulls up to the curb. "Why is it so crowded?"

I ask. "You'd think it was a Saturday night or something!"

"We can't go to movies on Saturday nights anymore, remember?" says Nanea. "There's the blackout—no lights on at night, especially downtown."

"Plus the curfew," adds Lily. "We can't be outside at night."

Nanea sighs. "The war changed *everything.*"

"Not everything," says Gene. "We can still catch a double feature for a dime. Who's ready?"

A *dime*? Sure enough, when we get close to the entrance, I see that admission is only ten cents. What a deal! But another poster says we can get in free if we buy something called a "War Bond" in the lobby.

Gene jingles his dimes in his hand as we step inside.

"Our school earned a Minuteman flag because so many students bought War Stamps," Nanea tells me. "Does your school sell stamps, too?"

"I, um . . . don't really understand the whole War Stamps thing," I admit.

"Oh! War Stamps and Bonds are sold to make money for the war. They're like special savings accounts. Papa says we loan money to our country, and then they'll pay us back with interest—more money—later on."

I still don't really get it, but I'm impressed that Nanea is loaning money to her country. That sounds very official. I loan money to my little brothers sometimes, but I'm pretty sure they'll never pay me back—and definitely not with interest!

We get inside just as the movie is starting. I've seen Sherlock Holmes movies before, but this one feels different right away. It's all about the war—Nazi spies, soldiers, and secret codes.

When the movie ends, I start to get out of my seat, but Nanea pulls me back down. "It's time for the news!"

Sure enough, there are five or ten minutes of news. It's all about the war. Planes dropping bombs. Tanks firing guns. It's black and white and feels very far away, until I remember where I am—or *when* I am. *This is all going on right now,* I remind myself. I'm relieved when the tanks and guns fade to black.

The next part of the news is about cryptologists. I'm about to ask Nanea if she knows what those are, but then I find out—they're people whose job it is to break top-secret codes. We learn that American cryptologists broke a top-secret Japanese code called JN-25.

"Look, some of the cryptologists are women!" Lily points out.

I don't usually get into the news, but this is pretty interesting stuff! I'm kind of disappointed when it ends. I get up again to leave, and Nanea says, "Where are you going?"

"Isn't it over?"

"No, silly. It's time for the next movie to start. It's a double feature!"

Another movie? And all for only ten cents! I happily plop back down to enjoy the show.

Turn to page 97.

I tried papaya for the first time today, and that went pretty well. So I agree to try hula, too.

"Hooray!" Nanea says, nearly flipping her plate of eggs. "What kind of story should we tell with our hula?"

My mind goes blank. Then I remember what Tutu said last night. She said that hula sometimes tells stories from long ago. And other times, hula tells stories that come from the heart.

I want Tutu to know that I heard her—and that I remember. But what kind of story do I want to tell?

It was fun watching Nanea and Mary Lou dance the story of Pele, the volcano goddess. But it might also be fun to make up a different kind of hula with Nanea.

To suggest a hula about Pele, turn to page 95.

To suggest a different kind of hula, turn to page 101.

an I drive you home?" asks Gene when we climb back into his car.

I nod with relief. "I live by the beach," I tell him.

Nanea, Lily, and I are all quiet as we drive. When Gene pulls up near the Royal Hawaiian Hotel, I hug both of my new friends good-bye. Then I hop out of the car and hurry toward the sand.

As soon as I'm alone, away from view, I lift the puka shell necklace off my head. The world spins, and my legs feel shaky all over again. But when the ground firms up beneath my feet, I can see my brothers. Relief washes over me like the surf itself. I'm home!

As my brothers finish up their sand castle, I sit down on my blanket and try to catch my breath. *Did that all really happen?* I wonder. *Or was it all a dream?*

When Aidan picks up a squirt gun and declares war on Alex, I shiver. I'm so glad my brothers don't have to worry about *real* war! They don't have to memorize Japanese bomber planes, or carry gas masks, or hide out in trenches during air-raid drills.

It's good we didn't go with Dad this time, I realize. And something else hits me, too. Dad didn't abandon us by going away. *He left us here to keep us safe!*

For the first time, I feel less lonely—and pretty lucky. I take a deep breath and then stretch out on my blanket, soaking up the sun and security of *home.*

The End

To read this story another way and see how different choices lead to a different ending, turn back to page 65.

Air raid?

My heart races as I search the sky. Are there planes coming? Are they dropping bombs? All I see are puffy white clouds.

Mrs. Watson comes flying into the garden. "Come on, girls," she says. "Grab your masks! Into the shelter!"

She squats in the yard beside the garden and pulls on a latch. A patch of sweet potato vines lifts right up out of the ground—like a trap door. There's a shelter built *into* the ground.

"Go on now," says Mrs. Watson, urging me down the ladder. My legs are weak, and it's dark and damp in the shelter. I can't see very well. But at least down here, maybe the planes can't see us either.

"Here, take Mele!" Nanea calls from above. As she lowers Mele down to me, the dog scrambles to get out. She scratches my arm, but I keep a firm grip on her.

"It's okay, girl," I whisper, even though *nothing* feels okay right now. I can barely breathe.

When Nanea climbs down and takes Mele from me, I don't want to let go. That's when Nanea sees how scared I am.

"I'm scared, too," she says. "I hope it's just a drill."

She buries her face in Mele's fur.

A drill? I sink to the dirt floor with relief.

"Yes, it probably is," says Mrs. Watson, lowering the roof overhead. Thin slivers of light outline the wooden trap door.

"But Mele doesn't like it any more than we do," says Nanea, holding her dog tight. "She doesn't like loud noises. On the day of the bombing, she ran away, and I didn't think we'd ever find her again." She strokes Mele's ears. "But do you know where she turned up?"

I shake my head.

"In a dirt shelter a little bit like this one. She fell in and got stuck. I had to pull her out. Isn't that right, silly poi dog?"

Mele whines and rests her chin on Nanea's arm.

I know just how you feel, I want to say. Sitting in this dark dugout, all I want to do is go home. My voice is shaky when I ask, "How do you know for sure it's just a drill?"

Nanea shakes her head. "We don't. That's the scariest part."

Mrs. Watson puts her hand on my shoulder. "We've had several drills, haven't we, girls?" she says. "Just to make sure we know what to do if another bomb is ever dropped. But I think we're safe. It'll be over soon."

I start to calm down, until something hops across my foot. "What was that?" I shriek, jumping up.

"What?" Nanea jumps up, too. Then she starts to laugh. "Oh, it's an island toad!" She points to the web-footed creature hiding in the shadows. "Leave it alone now, Mele."

The toad is *huge*. "It's as big as my foot!" I squeal. And I feel like its bumpy feet are still on me. I shake my body from head to toe, which makes Nanea giggle.

"See?" she says. "You *can* dance!"

That makes me laugh, too—until another siren sounds.

"It's all right," Mrs. Watson says quickly. "That's the all-clear signal. We can get out now." She pushes up on the trap door, and sunlight floods our dirt hole.

I don't know who wants to get out faster—me or Mele!

"You go first," says Nanea. "I'll hand her up to you."

I hurry up the ladder, leaving the toad and any other creepy-crawlies behind. Mele whines, but as soon as I'm back up on the grass, I realize something. The whining isn't coming from the hole. It's coming from the garden.

I whirl around and come face to face with two brown eyes—two *scared* brown eyes. It's another dog!

Turn to page 104.

"Let's keep going," says Lily. I wasn't sure she was on board with this mystery when it started, but now she seems determined to solve it.

"Wait," says Nanea. "I think we should review the facts first."

So we sit on the porch, and I open up the notebook. "I'm not so sure about Fact 3," says Lily. "If Anzu Sato is a neighbor, why don't I know her?"

"Right," says Nanea. "Good question."

"I guess I jumped to conclusions," I say. "Nancy Drew tries to never do that." I cross out Fact 3.

"I wish we had more evidence!" says Nanea. "But all we have is the book." She starts looking around the porch, as if something else might suddenly turn up.

I let my eyes wander, too, remembering how I spotted that book in a full stack this morning. It was on the bottom—one of the first books donated.

"Wait!" I say, jumping up. "Maybe Fact 1 is wrong, too. Maybe this book *didn't* come from a neighbor. Maybe it came from a Honolulu Helper!"

"Yes!" Nanea claps her hands, as if we've solved the mystery.

"But . . . we *know* all the club members," says Lily.

"And Anzu Sato isn't one of them."

She's right, I think, sitting back down. *Lily would make a good detective.*

Nanea's not ready to give up, though. "We should call every girl in our club. *Someone* must know something!"

Mrs. Suda lets us use the phone. It's clunky, with a big dial that spins. We take turns calling the Honolulu Helpers, one by one. Judy doesn't know anything. And Bernice isn't home. I get to call Audrey, which I'm happy about—she's the only girl in the club that I kind of got to know.

Her mother answers the phone with a thick accent. And then Audrey's quiet voice says, "Hello?"

I explain to her what we're doing—how we're trying to solve the mystery of the Nancy Drew book and the girl named Anzu.

That's when the line goes silent.

Turn to page 109.

A hula about Pele would be fun!" I say to Nanea. "Like the one you and Mary Lou did last night."

"You mean when I chased my little sister away?" jokes Mary Lou, taking a big bite of sausage.

Nanea laughs. "We were just playing around," she says. "Mary Lou and I weren't doing real hula. But you and I could. We could tell a story about Pele's journey to the volcanoes." Her hands start to move just thinking about it.

"I've never seen a volcano," I admit. The truth is, I'm kind of scared to get close to one. What if it erupts?

"Well, you must visit one," says Tutu, touching my hand. "It's difficult to do hula that speaks of things you haven't seen."

"I wish you could take us to the Punchbowl today, Papa," Nanea says. Then she whispers to me, "It's a big crater that was made when hot lava erupted."

Hot lava? I want to ask. *When?*

"I wish I could, too, Sunshine. But your poor old papa needs his beauty sleep after working the night shift." He yawns and stretches out his arms. "In fact, I think bed is calling to me right now." As he stands to leave, he kisses Nanea on the top of the head. "Maybe you could ask Uncle Fudge."

"Yes!" said Nanea. "Uncle Fudge did tell Lily that he would take us hiking sometime."

"Uncle Fudge?" I ask. I'm not crazy about volcanoes, but I *do* like fudge.

"Lily's dad," explains Nanea with a grin. "He's a fisherman. He used to take Lily and me out in his *sampan*, his boat, before the war. Maybe he could take us hiking up Punchbowl this morning!"

I try to smile, too, because she seems so excited. But the truth is, when I think of visiting a volcano today, fear starts bubbling up like hot lava, right inside my chest.

Turn to page 116.

e talk about cryptologists and secret codes all the way home.

"Our friend Donna wrote us a letter once that was kind of in secret code," says Nanea. "She lives in San Francisco now."

"She tore the letter in half and sent half to each of us," Lily explains. "We had to put them together to read it!"

"Speaking of secret code," says Gene, "I heard a rumor about a *dog* that could bark in Japanese code."

Nanea laughs and slaps the back of Gene's seat with her hand. "That's not true! We're not supposed to listen to rumors like that."

"Or spread them," Lily chimes in. "We could get in trouble for that. There are too many rumors going around the island right now."

"Like what?" I ask. I don't mean to gossip, but rumors about dogs that bark in code are pretty funny!

"Well," says Lily, "there was the one about how the Japanese poisoned our water."

Poison? I sink back in my seat. That doesn't sound funny at all.

"Or how about the one about our military firing at

an enemy submarine?" says Nanea. "It turned out to be a big school of fish!"

That one makes me laugh a little.

"The best one was about the secret warning hidden in the newspaper ad," says Gene.

Lily and Nanea start talking at the same time.

"It was an ad for nylon stockings, right?"

"That came out before the bombing of Pearl Harbor."

"So people said there were *clues* in it warning of the attack."

"Yeah, hidden clues. Like the black design in the corner of the ad was a cloud of smoke, and—"

"The word *parade* was in the ad, which rhymes with air raid."

"And the nylons were sold 'by the yard,' which meant *navy* shipyard."

"Was it all true?" I ask, getting sucked right in.

"No!" both girls say at the same time.

"None of it was true. But lots of people believed it," Nanea points out.

Huh. I wonder if I would have been one of those people, I think.

Before I know it, we're back at Lily's house. And Nanea asks me if I have to go home now.

Home? I'm not ready! I'm having too much fun here. So when Nanea asks if Lily and I want to do another sleepover—this time at her house—I can't say no.

Nanea uses Mrs. Suda's phone to call her mom and ask. When she and Lily come back from the kitchen, they both look discouraged.

"Did your mom say no?" I ask.

"My mom said yes," Nanea explains. "But Lily's mom says no."

Lily shrugs. "I have to babysit Tommy while my mom goes to a meeting. Hopefully *your* mom will say yes, though," she says.

My mom? Nanea wants me to call her right away. Luckily, she and Lily are out on the porch when I go into the kitchen to make the call. Mrs. Suda is standing at the sink, though, so I have to dial each number on the heavy black phone and wait for the dial to spin back around.

The phone doesn't ring—I know it won't, because Mom's phone number doesn't exist in the 1940s! But I know Mom isn't missing me. She's working, and my brothers are still building their sand castle.

I'm right where I want to be, too, I think.

Then I hurry outside to tell Nanea that I can stay another night. Woo-hoo!

Turn to page 112.

I think about how Nanea misses her brother and how I miss my dad. And I say, "Maybe our hula should tell a story about family."

Nanea smiles. "Yes. About *'ohana,* family."

So after Tutu and Tutu Kane leave, we clear our breakfast dishes. Then we go back into Nanea's room—David's old room—and we make up a hula about how much we miss our family.

"Maybe we should have the moon in our hula," says Nanea. "Because I know that wherever David is, he sees the same moon as I do. And then he doesn't seem so far away."

I smile. "It's like the ocean for me. I look out over the waves and pretend I see my dad's plane flying home."

Nanea nods thoughtfully. And with that, we begin to create our hula.

She teaches me the arm movements for *mahina,* or moon. "We're apart, but we see the same moon," she says, forming the shape of a moon with her arms. Her palms are turned up, with her fingertips touching.

Then we pretend we're palm trees on the beach, waving and waiting for our families to come home.

"Like this," says Nanea. She places the top of her left hand under her right elbow, and then sways her right hand like a palm tree in the breeze.

We finish by moving our hands up and down, showing the rhythm of the ocean. "They will return to us one day, like ocean waves," says Nanea. The thought of Dad coming home makes my eyes sting with tears, but Nanea pretends not to notice.

As we practice the dance, over and over, I start to feel better. We end our hula imagining that David and Dad have come home and we can wrap our arms around them. That part of the dance makes me so happy!

From sadness to happiness—I have so many emotions. *Thank goodness there's hula to help me say what's in my heart,* I think, giving Nanea a quick hug.

Turn to page 107.

t's okay," says Lily. "That's the all-clear siren. It's over now!"

I'm the last one to climb out of the trench. I want to make sure all the little kids get out first. Plus, I'm still afraid my legs won't work.

Nanea reaches out her hand to help me up. "You were so good with the kids!" she says, smiling. "You must do a great job babysitting your brothers."

I shrug. Helping with my brothers is a big job. *But I've never had to take care of them during an air-raid drill!* I want to say.

I picture little Annie crying in the dark, missing her mom. I'm so glad my brothers don't have to carry gas masks or worry about bomber planes. But I realize that they must miss Dad, too. I've been so worried about Dad that I never stopped to think about how it felt for my brothers to be without him. But maybe I can help them feel better, just like I did with Annie today.

As we walk back into the school, I make a promise to myself: I'll spend more time with my brothers when I go home.

Turn to page 119.

The rust-colored dog with floppy ears crouches beneath the mango tree, shaking. He has short little legs and a barrel chest, like a ripe, round mango that fell from the tree.

"It's okay," I say soothingly, holding out my hand. "Don't be afraid."

He whines and takes a step toward me. Then he takes two steps back.

"Oh, goodness!" says Mrs. Watson, climbing out of the shelter behind me.

"Is he yours?" I ask.

"No, I've never seen him before. But the poor thing is so scared."

"And so cute!" says Nanea, popping her head out of the shelter. "Mele, be nice now."

Mele's tail wags as she trots toward the dog to say hello. They touch noses and smell each other.

"I wonder if the siren scared him," says Nanea. "He probably ran away from his own yard."

"Do you think he lives near here?" I ask.

"Maybe," says Mrs. Watson. "We should try to find out. Why don't you girls take a break from gardening? I think this dog needs you right now more than I do."

I crouch next to him and hold out my hand again. Mele races over first to say hi to me, and the little dog follows, taking tiny careful steps. He sniffs my hand and looks up at me.

"It's okay," I say. "You can trust me."

He gives a little lick, as if to say, "I'll try." And then we're friends.

"C'mon, Mele!" calls Nanea as we set off down the street.

"C'mon . . . Mango!" I call to the other pup. The name seems to fit, and he trots toward us.

The four of us go door to door, ringing doorbells. Because it's Saturday, lots of neighbors are home. But no one seems to recognize Mango.

"Where does he belong?" Nanea says as we reach the end of another block. "We're almost back in my neighborhood!"

"I don't know," I say, squatting beside Mango. "I wish he were mine, though." I lean over low enough to get a wet kiss on the nose.

Nanea laughs. "He really likes you!"

"I think he knows we're trying to help him," I say, scratching behind one of his floppy ears. He sits down to make sure I have time to rub the other one, too. Then he bites a string dangling from my cover-up.

"Oh, I wonder if he's hungry!" says Nanea. "Let's go home for lunch and feed him something."

Turn to page 124.

hen we're ready to perform our hula, Nanea cracks her bedroom door and peeks outside. Then she ducks back in. "Papa's awake!" she says.

As we tiptoe into the living room, he reaches out to tickle her. "There's my sunshine!" he says. "I was afraid it was going to be a cloudy day."

Nanea wraps her arms around his neck and squeezes. She asks her father if he'd like to see our hula.

"I thought you'd never ask." Mr. Mitchell settles back onto the couch.

I'm nervous to dance in front of him, until he wiggles his eyebrows at me. That's just how my dad would make me smile!

Nanea tells him what we're doing as we dance—about the moon that David sees that's just like ours. About the palm trees waiting and waving on shore. And about the waves that will bring our loved ones home again.

Mr. Mitchell wipes his eyes when we finish. He must miss David an awful lot, too. But then he whistles, claps, and cheers—until Nanea giggles and says, "Okay, that's enough, silly Papa."

When it's time for Nanea to leave for gardening, I

know it's time for me to go home, too. Only now there's someone new for me to miss: Nanea.

Her dad offers to drive me home, which I say is near Waikiki Beach. As we climb into the back of his car, Nanea says sadly, "I know you and your family are leaving soon. I'm going to miss you!"

I make the arm motions for "moon." "Just look up," I tell her. "And I will, too."

She smiles and curves her own arms into a moon.

I want to freeze that picture of Nanea—to remember her always. And that's when I make a decision.

I'm going to take hula lessons, like Mom wants me to. It might help me make new friends. But mostly, I hope it'll help me remember the one who is sitting beside me right now.

The End

To read this story another way and see how different choices lead to a different ending, turn back to page 69.

udrey? Are you there?" I think we got cut off, but then I hear her. She's *crying*.

"Can I come over?" she asks.

Our mystery just got a whole lot more mysterious, I think as I hang up the phone.

Audrey shows up about fifteen minutes later. Her eyes are red and her cheeks tear-stained. "Are you okay?" asks Nanea, reaching for her hand.

Audrey takes a deep, shaky breath and sits down on the steps beside us. "I know who Anzu Sato is," she says.

"Who?" we ask.

"She's *me*," says Audrey. "I changed my name after the war started, because . . ." Her voice trails off.

"Because you're Japanese, like me," says Lily softly. "I understand." She puts her arm around Audrey.

It seems like I'm the only one who *doesn't* understand. "Wait, why would you change your name?"

"Because of how badly the Japanese are being treated!" says Nanea. "Lots of Japanese men were arrested because people thought they might be spies. Even Lily's dad."

"Mr. Suda?" I ask.

Nanea nods. "He got to come home again, but some Japanese men didn't. They got sent to a detention camp called Sand Island. They're still there."

"And Daddy says it's awful there," says Lily.

Audrey suddenly starts crying all over again. She wipes the tears with the back of her hand and says, "My dad is at Sand Island."

"Oh, no!" says Lily.

Audrey nods. "We're scared he's going to be sent back to the mainland. My whole family is being treated like we're the enemy. So my mom said we should change our names to sound less Japanese. She won't wear her kimono. We don't even speak Japanese in our house anymore."

I don't know what to say. I feel sick to my stomach. Then I think of Audrey's dad again. "Is this a picture of him?" I ask, sliding the photo out of the book.

Audrey nods. "It's him and me. I can't believe I almost gave that away!" She takes the photo and presses it to her chest. Then she reaches for the book and stands up. "Thank you for finding these for me."

Before we can stop her, she starts to walk down the sidewalk. "Audrey?" I say, jumping up quickly.

When she turns, I say, "I really like the name Anzu. It's unique—and so pretty."

She smiles. "It means apricot. My dad picked it out." Then her face falls. "But Audrey is better now," she says firmly before walking away.

Turn to page 130.

live right down the street," Nanea tells me. "We can walk!"

So we say good-bye to Lily, and then we head off down the street. Nanea tells me all about her family as we go. Her dad works as a welder at the Pearl Harbor shipyard. Her mom helps out with the Red Cross. Her older sister, Mary Lou, is . . .

"Well, she's hard to explain." Nanea laughs. "But you'll meet her! And then there's my brother, David. But you already know about him."

She gets really quiet. But when we hear a dog bark, she perks back up. "And then there's Mele!"

A scruffy dog bounds off a porch and races toward us. I recognize her right away—she's the dog I saw with Nanea outside the Royal Hawaiian Hotel!

"Oh, silly dog. I missed you last night!" Nanea crouches low for a kiss.

When I kneel beside her, Mele sniffs and licks my hand, too. What a sweetie!

"Does Mom have dinner cooking?" asks Nanea. "Let's follow our noses, Mele."

The three of us hurry up the porch steps and into the house. But as we step into the living room, Nanea stops short. There's a soldier on the couch, and I can tell she doesn't recognize him.

"Good, Nanea, you're home," says a woman, wiping her hands on her apron as she steps into the room. "This is Lieutenant Foster."

He has cropped dark hair and a shy smile. When he stands to greet us, I'm surprised by how tall he is.

"Papa and I invited him here for dinner and a night or two away from base. He has a weekend pass. We thought he could sleep in David's room. Can you and your friend sleep on the daybed or in Mary Lou's room?"

Nanea nods. But as we head into the kitchen, she whispers to me, "Mary Lou snores."

I smother a laugh—and I'm glad I do, because Mary Lou is setting the table in the kitchen. She has Nanea's same dark hair.

"Just in time!" says Mary Lou, handing Nanea a stack of plates. She's humming to herself and does a little twirl as she grabs cloth napkins from the counter.

"You're in a good mood," says Nanea. "Wait, I bet I know why. Does it have something to do with a cute soldier joining us for dinner?"

Mary Lou's jaw drops open. "Nanea!" she whispers, swatting her with a napkin. "Keep your voice down."

By the way Mary Lou is smiling, I think Nanea might be on to something here.

During dinner, Lieutenant Foster is super quiet. Nanea's mom and dad ask him lots of questions about his family and his home. But no one pays more attention to him than Mary Lou.

Nanea nudges me every time Mary Lou passes the soldier the potatoes or refills his water. She gives me a knowing look, like, "See? I told you!"

One time, Mary Lou catches us spying on her, but she doesn't get mad. She just winks.

After dinner, we take Mele out for a quick walk. "Can you believe Mary Lou?" says Nanea as we leap off the back porch. "She's already sweet on Lieutenant Foster. I hope I'm not like that when I'm her age."

Me, too, I'm about to say. But when Mele stops to take a drink from a water bowl next to the garage, something catches my eye—a scrap of bright yellow paper on the ground. It's tucked under the tire of the bicycle leaning against the side of the house.

As I slide the paper out, I realize that it's not a scrap

at all—it's a tiny bird! And it looks as if there's something written on its wings.

"An origami crane!" says Nanea when I show her. "Unfold it and see what it says."

I start to unfold the paper, but I can't make myself do it. The little bird is so perfectly folded. "I'll never be able to fold it up again," I say. "And it's so cute."

"I can refold it," Nanea tells me. "I know how to do origami—Lily's mom taught me. So open it up and see what it says. I'm so curious!"

Now I am, too. I carefully unfold the little wings. I smooth the paper flat against the side of the house. And when I see what's written on it, I suck in my breath.

It's a message—written in *secret code.*

Turn to page 121.

An hour later, we're hiking up a steep dirt trail. I'm still nervous about seeing Punchbowl Crater. But that doesn't take my mind off the smell drifting out of Nanea's basket. "Do I smell guava bread?" I ask.

Lily giggles. "You sound just like Donna!" she says.

"Your friend who moved away?" I ask.

Nanea nods. "She has a sweet tooth. She'd do anything for guava bread. And she was almost always with us. Papa called us the Three Kittens."

"Meow," says Lily. "I miss Donna."

"Meow, too," says Nanea with a sad little laugh.

Me, too, I almost say, suddenly picturing Kayla's face. Hiking with Nanea and Lily is fun, but it makes me miss my old friend a little, too.

"Do I hear kittens following us up the trail?" asks Uncle Fudge, who is in the lead. He has Lily's shiny black hair and a warm smile.

Lily laughs. "No, Daddy—it's just us. But are we almost there?"

"Almost," he says. "But the last stop is not the only one to think of. You should enjoy the whole journey. Stop to admire the blossoms."

As Uncle Fudge points out a cluster of tiny flowers on a nearby bush, I take the opportunity to set down my gas mask—the one I borrowed from David. It's really heavy. I can't believe people had to carry these everywhere during the war. Even while hiking!

Nanea sets her picnic basket down, too, and pretty soon we're all resting, gazing at the valley below. The trail we just hiked cuts through groves of squat bushes and trees, and even some prickly cactus. Uncle Fudge points out a few goats roaming on a nearby hillside, and as if on cue, one of them bleats at us.

"Is he telling us to stop and smell the flowers, Uncle Fudge?" asks Nanea, giggling.

"Maybe," says Uncle Fudge with a wink. "But the flowers aren't all I smell right now." He casts a sideways glance at Nanea's basket. "Are there any oatmeal cookies in there?" He raises his eyebrows hopefully.

She laughs and opens the basket. "Of course!"

Uncle Fudge takes a cookie, and I sink my teeth into a slice of guava bread. It tastes like Auntie Oli's. *I hope Mom gets the recipe,* I think, *so we can still have it after we leave Hawaii.*

Looking out over that beautiful valley, I realize

there *are* some things I'll miss when we go. Like guava bread. And my new friends. And the beauty of the island.

But definitely not volcanoes.

Turn to page 127.

Instead of going back to Lily's, I decide it's time to go home. I miss my little brothers *so* much right now!

Gene offers to drive me back to the beach, where I tell him I'll meet my family. As he pulls up in front of the Royal Hawaiian Hotel, I give Lily and Nanea big hugs.

"So tell me," says Nanea with a grin, "how many shells *are* in your necklace?"

"I don't know!" I hold it away from my chest, trying to count.

She laughs. "The number doesn't matter. It's full of aloha—like you. You really helped those kids feel better today."

I shake my head. "I'm not so sure about that. I was pretty scared, too."

"We all were. But that's aloha!" Nanea says. "Helping someone else *even* when you're scared."

This time, I think I know what my new friend means. *Is that how she stays so brave?* I wonder. *By helping other people?*

As the car pulls away, Nanea and Lily wave and wave. I wait till the car turns back onto the main street.

Then I walk toward the beach.

My walk turns into a run. I can't wait to see my brothers! I find the hole in the barbed-wire fence. I take my puka shell necklace and gently pull it over my head. I feel warm with aloha from my head to my toes.

There they are! My brothers are still building that sand castle with Auntie Oli. Only now, I'm going to help them, too.

"Alex! Aidan! Can I take a turn?"

Alex grins and hands me his cup.

As I scoop it into the cool, wet sand, I ask my brothers, "How high do you think we can make this tower? Ten cups high? Or maybe twelve?"

"Seventeen!" says Alex.

"A gazillion million!" says Aidan.

Auntie Oli laughs and walks back toward her towel. She must know that I'm going to play with my brothers for a while. Because that's my job.

The End

To read this story another way and see how different choices lead to a different ending, turn back to page 34.

The capital letters are tiny, written in black ink with perfect handwriting. But they don't make sense. Odd combinations of letters are grouped together, with spaces in between.

"It's definitely written in code," whispers Nanea. "Where did you find it again?"

I point toward the wheel of the bike. "Is that your dad's?"

Nanea shakes her head. "That must be Lieutenant Foster's bike. Which means . . . this must be Lieutenant Foster's message. But who would he be writing to in code?"

I say the first thing that comes to mind. "A spy?"

Nanea doesn't look so sure. When Mele lets out a yelp, Nanea reaches down to scratch the dog's ears. "Sorry, girl. Let's get walking."

I study the code as we circle the block, but I can't figure it out. "I think we need some kind of decoder."

"Let me try." Nanea takes the note, but she can't make sense of it either.

When we get back to the house, I put the message in my pocket. I can't stop thinking about it, though—and about Lieutenant Foster. Could he be a spy? *He's awfully quiet,* I remember. *Maybe he does have something to hide.*

At bedtime, Nanea and I sleep on what her mom called the "daybed." It looks like an orange futon with one long cushion, and it pulls out into a double bed. When I'm snuggled underneath the quilt with the bright blue flowers, I feel cozy and warm. I like knowing Nanea is right there—especially with my mind swirling about enemy spies and secret codes.

I fall asleep listening to the snoring coming from Mary Lou's room. And then something wakes me with a start—the creak of a bedroom door. Is it Mary Lou?

I try to make out the shadowy figure in the dark. It's much too tall to be Mary Lou. It must be Lieutenant Foster.

He crosses the room slowly, taking quiet, steady steps. *Is he coming toward us?* The hair stands up on my arms. But, no—he's going toward the front door. He eases it open and steps outside.

"Where's he going?" Nanea's whisper breaks the silence. "He can't go out there. It's after curfew!"

There's a wartime rule that no one can be outside after dark. But even without a curfew, it's pretty weird that Lieutenant Foster would leave in the middle of the night. And by the way he was tiptoeing, he sure didn't want us to know he was going!

Now I'm wide awake—and Nanea is, too. But when the front door opens an hour or so later, we both pretend to be asleep. And that mysterious soldier goes right back into the bedroom, as if he'd never been gone.

Turn to page 132.

ango's belly is round by the time we're done eating. He curls up in a happy little ball.

"Now he really *does* look like a ripe, round mango," says Nanea. "I think he likes sausage almost as much as Mele does!"

I'm full, too, as I eat the last bite of my peanut butter and guava jelly sandwich. Mrs. Mitchell takes my plate. "It's kind of you to try to find Mango's home," she says to me. "But are your parents going to want *you* home soon, too?"

I shake my head. "Not yet," I say. "I can stay a little longer." A part of me worries that we won't find Mango's owner today. But another part of me worries that we *will*—too soon. I'm not ready to say good-bye!

"Look," says Nanea as we step outside again. "There's Auntie Rose! Maybe she'll recognize Mango."

A woman sits sipping a cold drink on her front porch. She's wearing a loose dress called a *mu'umu'u*. I only know that because Auntie Oli sometimes wears that same style. As I follow Nanea across the red dirt yard, I whisper, "Is Auntie Rose your mother's sister?" She has dark hair like Nanea and her mother.

Nanea shakes her head. "She's my auntie because

I have known her my whole life. She's like my family. She isn't my babysitter, but she does take care of me, in a way."

Like Auntie Oli, I realize.

"Ah, there's my favorite neighbor," calls Auntie Rose as we get closer. "With a new friend. And a new four-legged friend, too!"

Nanea introduces us and asks if Auntie Rose has ever seen Mango before. "Hmm," she says. "No. But there are many stray dogs on Oahu now, with families being sent back to the mainland."

"You think he doesn't have a home?" says Nanea with alarm.

My chest tightens, too. Did someone leave this little pup behind? How *could* they?

"I don't know," says Auntie Rose gently. "Families have to leave so quickly—when the government says so."

"Like Donna and her mom did," says Nanea sadly. "I know. But who will take care of the animals that get left behind?"

Auntie Rose tucks a strand of hair behind Nanea's ear. "You will," she says with a smile. "If this dog has a home, you will find it. You will *kokua* and help him. And I will help *you*. I'll let our neighbors know."

Nanea's face relaxes. "Thank you, Auntie Rose."

We stay for a glass of guava juice—Auntie Rose insists. She brings out Portuguese sausages for Mele and Mango, too. I can't believe Mango is still hungry after his big lunch!

Nanea bends down to scratch Mango's ears. "Auntie Rose is taking good care of you, isn't she, little dog? Together, we'll find your home."

I hope so, I think. I hope Mango wasn't abandoned, left behind when his family went overseas. *Like me, when Dad left.*

Maybe that's why I already love Mango so much. We're both a little lost without the people we love.

Turn to page 136.

C'mon, crew," says Uncle Fudge as he swallows his last bite of cookie. "Time to move on."

As we near the top, my stomach flops like a fish. Will we actually see a volcano? Or feel its heat?

I'm surprised—and relieved—when we don't! Instead, I can see Oahu in all directions. The city of Honolulu. Waikiki Beach. Green valleys, and more mountains in the distance. And the ocean stretching out for miles. I feel like I can see all the way to the bottom of the clear turquoise water. It's so beautiful!

Standing beside me, Uncle Fudge shades his eyes and takes a deep breath, as if drinking in the air.

"Daddy, are you thinking about fishing?" asks Lily, leaning her head against him.

He sighs. "A little bit, dear one. I was thinking about the Japanese fishermen who had their sampans taken away—and never returned. See the white boat?" He points. "I think that's a sampan that has been painted. The military is patrolling the shore with it now."

"Wait, why were their boats taken away?" I ask Nanea.

She shivers. "Because after Japan bombed Pearl Harbor, our government thought anyone from Japan could be a spy. They thought Japanese fishermen might be meeting enemy submarines in their sampans. The FBI arrested Uncle Fudge just because he's Japanese!" Her eyes flash with anger.

"But I'm home now," says Uncle Fudge, squeezing Nanea's shoulder. Then he points past Honolulu toward a greenish-brown mountain with a flat top. "Who can tell me about *Leahi*?" he asks, changing the subject.

"I can!" says Lily. "We call it Leahi because it's shaped like a fish, like a long ahi tuna."

"But the crater is *also* called Diamond Head," Nanea points out. "Tutu Kane says it's because sailors thought they saw diamonds glittering at the top."

"Right," says Uncle Fudge. "You listen well to Tutu Kane's stories."

"Wait, *that's* the volcano?" I say, laughing with relief. "It's so far away! I thought we would get closer to a volcano today."

Nanea gives me a strange look. "Well, we did just climb out of one," she says. She points back at the trail.

When I look down, I see it for the first time: the bowl-shaped crater. "We were *inside* a volcano?"

"Yes!" she says, laughing. "Inside Punchbowl."

I feel foolish now—but also relieved. "I thought there would be more fire or lava or something."

"The last eruption was nearly one hundred thousand years ago," Uncle Fudge says. "But if you want to be *truly* safe, you should pay your respects to Pele, the volcano goddess." He winks.

"Yes!" says Nanea. "If you see an old woman with long white hair, you must greet her with aloha."

"And offer her food and flowers!" chimes in Lily. "Except I think you ate all the guava bread."

That makes me laugh. I don't know anyone with long white hair—except maybe Auntie Oli. But I search the valley below, wondering if we might see Pele today. Goose bumps pop up on my arms, and I brush them away before anyone sees.

It's one thing to be scared of volcanoes. I don't want my new friends to know that I'm scared of volcano *goddesses*, too!

Turn to page 134.

"Well, I guess we solved the mystery."

I sink back onto the steps beside Nanea.

"And there *was* a crime." She gives the dirt an angry kick. "They sent her dad away just because he's Japanese. But that doesn't make him a spy."

Lily puts her face in her hands. "Poor Audrey! She must miss her dad so much. How can we help her?"

I think of how Audrey was helping us this morning, collecting books and magazines for wounded soldiers—other people's fathers. "Maybe," I say slowly, "we can send something to her dad."

"What do you mean?" Lily perks up.

"I don't know. Maybe some books to take his mind off where he is?"

"And cookies," says Nanea. "Like we brought your dad when they took him away."

Lily nods. "We might still have some from the cookie giveaway," she says. "Let's ask my mom!" She jumps up and hurries inside.

Mrs. Suda is chopping vegetables in the kitchen. "You girls must be starving," she says with a smile.

But when we tell her our idea, she sets down the knife and puts her arm around Lily. "I don't know if the guards will let Mr. Sato have the package," she says. "But it's a very kind idea. You could give it to Audrey and her mother—and hope for the best."

Lily, Nanea, and I lock eyes and smile. At least we have a plan, some small way to help our new friend Audrey.

Turn to page 138.

When Nanea and I wake up the next morning, Lieutenant Foster is gone. The door to David's bedroom is wide open, and the bed is made.

When we bring Mele outside, the soldier's bike is gone, too.

"Look!" Nanea points to a bit of orange paper on the ground near where the bike used to be. She shows me a tiny folded lizard. "It's a gecko. An origami gecko."

We both see the writing on the gecko's leg. But before we can unfold it, someone calls to Nanea. An older woman with a cane is hurrying toward us.

"Good morning, Mrs. Lin," says Nanea, folding her fingers around the gecko.

"Good morning, Nanea. How is your mother today? I saw you had company last night. Poor soldier—so far from home. He must have enjoyed your mother's cooking. Did she make her shoyu chicken? What a delicious dish. Maybe you could get the recipe for me."

"Yes, Mrs. Lin."

Those are the only three words Nanea can get out before Mrs. Lin starts talking again. "What's in your hand? Origami? Let me see. So tiny!"

As Nanea unfolds her hand, Mrs. Lin reaches for

the gecko. "Did you write on it?" She holds it up to the morning light. "I don't understand. What does it say?"

Nanea turns to me, like she's not sure how much to tell Mrs. Lin. I'm not sure either. If Lieutenant Foster *is* a spy, we have to tell someone! But how can we know for sure?

To tell Mrs. Lin about the spy, turn to page 143.

To say something about the secret message, turn to page 147.

Do you see the old cars?" asks Nanea, pointing to a field in the distance. We're still sitting at the top of the crater, enjoying the amazing view.

"Yes. That's weird. What are they doing there?" The field looks like a junkyard, or a strange mountainside parking lot.

"The jalopies are put in open fields to keep enemy planes from landing," says Uncle Fudge. "Just like barbed wire was rolled out on beaches to keep enemy boats from coming ashore."

So *that's* why the barbed wire is on the beach! It all makes sense to me now. But I feel a shiver of fear. Just when I start to forget the war and enjoy my time with Nanea, something happens to remind me.

As I look back at Punchbowl, I suddenly feel silly, worrying about volcanoes. These craters haven't erupted in one hundred thousand years! But a war is going on right here in Oahu, right *now.*

How can something so awful happen in such a beautiful place? I wonder. *And how can Nanea live with being scared all the time?*

There she is, offering Lily a pretty wildflower blossom that she found on the ground as if she were paying her respects to Pele. *Showing her aloha,* I think, *just like she has shown me. Is that how she stays so positive?*

I know it hasn't been easy for Nanea, though. She hides in the closet during blackouts, and she worries for David at night. I worry about my dad a lot, too. But at least the war he's fighting is somewhere else instead of here at home.

Home? I catch myself. I've never called Hawaii home before! But I've never climbed a volcano before either. Or eaten papaya. Or made up a hula dance with my friends. So I say it again in my mind. *Home.*

Turn to page 141.

When we see a mailman across the street, Mele barks hello. The man looks toward us and waves.

"That's Mr. Cruz," says Nanea. "He knows everyone in the neighborhood, so maybe he knows Mango!" She jumps up and hurries down the porch steps.

But Mr. Cruz doesn't recognize the dog either. "I would remember," says the mailman with a thick accent. "He looks like a *salsicha*."

Nanea laughs. "That's Portuguese for 'sausage,'" she tells me.

"Do you want to draw a picture?" asks Mr. Cruz. "I can take it on my route—show the neighbors. Maybe someone will remember this little salsicha."

"Yes!" says Nanea. "We could make posters—one for you and more to hang up around the neighborhood. We did that when Mele was missing."

So we hurry back to Nanea's room, where she pulls out a box of paper and crayons from under her bed. Mango lies on the bed beside us, the perfect model.

"I wish I were a better artist," I say, finishing my first picture of the pup.

"That's pretty good!" says Nanea. "He *does* kind of

look like a sausage, doesn't he?"

I turn the picture sideways, and I have to admit that he does.

My next picture looks better than the first. And by my tenth poster, I've drawn the perfect Mango. He's standing up, and I drew little lines by his tail to make it look like it's wagging. His eyes are big, brown, and round. They look out from the poster as if to say, "Take me home!"

I wish I could, buddy. I turn to pet the real Mango, who is curled up in a ball on the floor.

"Do you think we've made enough posters?" I ask, shaking out my cramped hand.

"I think so," says Nanea. "Let's give one to Mr. Cruz and then put up the rest around the neighborhood."

She pulls the stapler out of her craft box and hurries to tell her mom what we're doing. Then we head out the door again, with two dogs on our heels.

Turn to page 144.

"Where did you get these again?" asks Lily as she slides a few magazines into the bottom of a box.

"They were David's," says Nanea. "I mean, they still are. But now that he's in the army, maybe he won't miss them."

She holds on to the last magazine for a long time before setting it down. I can tell she's thinking about her brother—and missing him the way I miss Dad.

"You were right," I say softly. "When we were rolling bandages, you said that when you miss your brother, it makes you feel better to have something to do—to help other people. You were right about that, Nanea. I miss my dad, but it makes me feel better to help Audrey's dad right now."

She doesn't say anything, but she smiles wide and gives me a quick hug. Then she adds a few more magazines to the box.

Lily puts some books in, too, donated by her dad. And on top she sets some cookies, wrapped in wax paper.

"That's it!" she says. "And just in time. Audrey and her mom will be here any minute."

When the doorbell rings, I'm so nervous! I hope

Audrey likes what we did for her. And I hope she and her mom can find a way to get it to her dad.

Audrey's mother and Mrs. Suda talk on the porch while Audrey steps inside. "This is for me?" she asks, opening the box.

"Actually, it's for your dad," says Nanea.

Audrey's eyes fill with tears when she sees what's inside. "He loves mochi," she whispers.

"There are Portuguese malasadas, and Hawaiian guava bread, and Chinese crack seed, too," says Nanea, pointing. "Lots of different treats and flavors. From all the different kinds of people who live here in Hawaii."

"Like at our cookie giveaway," says Lily.

"Like miso soup!" I say.

The other girls look at me and laugh.

"You know what I mean," I say. "It's good to have lots of different flavors coming together."

Nanea nods. "We're *all* different here in Hawaii. But we also have a lot in common. We all love Hawaii. It's our home."

"*And* . . . we all love Nancy Drew mysteries," I remind Audrey.

That makes her smile.

"Should we seal the box?" asks Lily.

Audrey hesitates. "I want to add one more thing. May I borrow a pen?"

Lily disappears into the kitchen. When she comes back, she hands Audrey a pen. Then Audrey pulls something out of her pocket—the photo of her and her dad. She places it on the coffee table facedown and writes something on the back.

I can't read the whole message, but I see the way she signs her name—in big letters. "Anzu."

Turn to page 150.

I'm surprised by how fun it is to make up a hula about Pele, now that I have visited Punchbowl.

"Can we show how we hiked up the steep mountain trail like Pele did?" I ask.

"Yes, with the kaholo," says Nanea. She slides her feet side to side and then diagonally, as if moving up the zigzagging trail.

I'm nervous to try it at first. But Lily tells me that she's never taken formal hula lessons either. She's a beginner, like me!

"We should tell about the beautiful view when we got to the top!" says Lily.

"Yes, with the *huli*!" says Nanea. She rotates in a circle while swaying her hips. She makes it look easy, but it's not. Lily and I try it, and every time we turn and catch each other's eye, we burst out laughing.

Then Nanea teaches us hand movements to talk about the ocean that we saw from the top of the volcano. Our hands gently beat up and down, like ocean waves.

"And when the ocean is angry, it rolls like this!" Nanea rolls her hands over each other to show rough waters.

Doing hula for the first time feels strange—but fun! I even start to make up moves of my own. When I shade my eyes, as if enjoying the view at the top of Punchbowl, Lily asks me if I've seen any lava yet. She laughs, teasing me like a good friend would.

"I'm scared of volcanoes," I admit. "But dancing makes me feel less scared." I wonder if that's Nanea's secret. Does hula help her forget the war? Does it make her feel less scared?

Turn to page 157.

As soon as I decide to tell Mrs. Lin what's going on, the words practically spill out of my mouth.

"We didn't write this note. We think Lieutenant Foster did. He might be a spy!"

"Who?" asks Mrs. Lin, shocked.

"The soldier who stayed with us last night." Nanea keeps her voice low and looks over her shoulder, as if the lieutenant might be standing there.

Mrs. Lin clucks her tongue. "And after you took him in and gave him a place to sleep!" She shakes her head. "No one can be trusted during this war."

"But we don't know for sure!" Nanea says quickly. "Please don't tell anyone yet."

"Of course," says Mrs. Lin. "Well, I'd better go, Nanea. Be careful now." But instead of going back toward her own yard, she crosses the street.

"Oh no," whispers Nanea. "She's going to see Mrs. Santos. If Mrs. Lin tells her what we said, *everyone* in the neighborhood will know!"

Now I'm worried, too. Because . . . what if we're wrong about Lieutenant Foster?

Turn to page 153.

I'm dragging my feet by the time we've stapled up our last poster. We must have walked every inch of Nanea's neighborhood, putting posters on each corner. And then we walked through some of the surrounding neighborhoods, too.

"My feet hurt from walking!" I tell Nanea as we head inside for dinner.

"Mine, too," she says. "But it was worth it. Someone will know Mango. I'm sure of it."

Mango seems to think so, too. He whines by the door after dinner, as if waiting for his owners to come and pick him up.

"You two had better take the dogs out one more time," says Mrs. Mitchell. She's already covering the windows with blankets for the blackout.

We take the dogs for a walk around the block, watching the neighbors covering their windows, one by one. As we're about to turn back onto Nanea's street, a woman calls to us.

"It's Mrs. Santos," says Nanea. "I wonder what she wants?"

The woman waves us toward her yard with a yellow dish towel, as if she was in the middle of washing dishes when we passed by.

"Come," says Mrs. Santos. "I have something to tell you." When she spots Mango, her tan face breaks into a grin. "Ah, this is the pup Rose told me about."

"Do you know him?" asks Nanea hopefully.

Mrs. Santos shakes her head. "I know Mrs. Ikeda, who has a neighbor named Mrs. Alana, who has a daughter named Sukey, who lives over on King and Kaheka. Sukey's family is missing a puppy like this one. It is a very sad family over on King Street."

"We were just on King Street!" says Nanea. "It's not far from Mrs. Watson's," she explains to me.

"And maybe you will go back tomorrow," says Mrs. Santos. "To return this one to his family." She pats Nanea's arm. "You're a good girl." Then Mrs. Santos disappears back into her house.

"Tomorrow?" says Nanea. "If we wait until tomorrow, Mango will miss his family tonight. And they'll be so worried about him!"

"Should we take him home?" I ask, even though I can't bear the thought of saying good-bye to Mango.

Nanea hesitates. "We could. It's not far, so we'll be home before curfew. But . . . if you want to wait until morning to bring Mango home, I'll understand."

I stare into Mango's trusting eyes. "What do you think we should do?" I ask him.

He offers me his paw, and that helps me decide.

To take Mango home tonight,
go online to **beforever.com/endings**

To wait until morning,
turn to page 155.

t's written in a secret code," I say, because that's kind of obvious.

Mrs. Lin's eyebrows raise. "I love secrets!" she says. "What does it say?"

She taps her cane on the sidewalk, waiting for us to tell her. But the truth is, we don't know what the message says. So Nanea offers to go get that chicken recipe for her, and we hurry back to Nanea's house.

"What *does* it say? I'm dying to know!" I say when we're out of earshot.

"We're going to have to break the code. C'mon." Nanea leads me into the backyard, which looks and smells like a flower shop.

We duck down between the fence and a bush filled with waxy leaves and red blossoms. Mele squeezes in, too, and lies down on her belly for a morning nap.

Then Nanea unfolds the gecko and smooths it out against the fence. I pull the other message from my pocket, and we hold them up side by side. The code written on the gecko looks just like the other one: tiny capital letters separated into groups, like words.

"Do you recognize any of the words?" I ask.

She narrows her eyes, studying them. "No. But what

are the most common words? Maybe we can figure out some of the short ones, like *and* or *the*."

"Oh, that's smart. There's a three-letter word." I point to a group of three letters in the first row of her message. It reads W-O-H.

"So maybe a *W* is really an *A*, and *O* is an *N*, and *H* is a *D*." Nanea pauses. "Boy, it'll take a long time to figure out the code this way."

"Or *maybe*," I say, studying the word again, "the words are all written backward! W-O-H might really be the word *how*. See?"

"Yeah!" Nanea gets excited, until she looks at the other words. "That's the only word that works that way, though. Wait!" When she jumps straight up, Mele whines. "Maybe the words are scrambled! We need pencils."

While she runs into the house, I study the message on the crane. I move the first few letters around until they form a word: *when*. By the time Nanea comes back, I have the first nine words unscrambled. "When I grow up, I want to be a . . ."

"Really?" Nanea hands me a pencil. "You want to talk about jobs right now?"

"No!" I say, laughing. "That's what my message says! But I can't get the next word. It's super long."

Nanea studies it over my shoulder. It takes us a long time to finally figure it out. "Cryptologist!" Nanea says.

We quickly unscramble the last three words. The full message reads: *When I grow up, I want to be a cryptologist. How about you?*

"What a weird message. A kid must have written it, but the handwriting is so perfect!" says Nanea. "Let's try mine now."

Together, we unscramble the message on the gecko. It reads: *Does Mele know how to bark in code? Maybe "bark" means "fish, please!"*

"Remember the rumor about dogs barking in code?" I say.

"Yeah, but who knows about that?" Nanea scratches her chin. "Just you, me, Gene, and . . ."

❀ ***Turn to page 162.***

fter Audrey and her mom go home, Mr. Suda offers to drive me home, too. And now I feel ready.

"What are you thinking about?" asks Nanea. She's sitting on one side of me in the backseat of the car, and Lily is on the other.

I tell her the truth. "I was thinking about my dad. I really miss him. But it's worse for Audrey—I mean Anzu. Her dad is being treated like a criminal!"

"I think we helped him today," says Nanea. "Or at least we tried."

"We helped a lot of soldiers this weekend," says Lily quietly. "Think of all the bandages we rolled."

"And books we collected!" says Nanea.

It's true. My new friends and I accomplished a lot with the Honolulu Helpers today, and had a lot of fun, too. And that gets me thinking about the Acts of Kindness project I started with Kayla back in California.

Can I start one again? I wonder. It won't be the same without Kayla, but maybe I'll meet some new friends, like I did today. I already know what our first project would be. We could make care packages for soldiers who are stationed far away—like Dad!

I spend the rest of the drive thinking about what I'd put in Dad's package. Pictures of me and my brothers, for sure. And some of Mom's chocolate chip cookies.

Mr. Suda takes me back to Waikiki Beach, where I tell him I'm going to meet my family. It's hard to say good-bye to my new friends, but now I'm excited to get back home. There's so much I want to do!

When I get to the beach, I hurry to the barbed-wire fence and step through. Then I carefully slide off the puka shell necklace, and cross my fingers that my family will be right where I left them.

The first person I see is Auntie Oli, steadying the sand castle before it tips into the ocean waves. My brothers are busily packing sand into cups to make it even *taller.*

"Auntie Oli!" I race toward her. I have a burning question to ask.

"Yes, child?" she says, turning toward me.

"Can we make some of your guava bread to send to Dad?"

She smiles warmly. "Of course! We'll bake some fresh today."

Then another question tumbles out of my mouth. "Do you know how to make mochi? Japanese mochi?"

Her eyes widen in surprise. "I do," she says. "It's one of my favorites."

Perfect! I think. Then I smile back. "Mine, too."

The End

To read this story another way and see how different choices lead to a different ending, turn back to page 70.

Nanea and I haven't even finished our breakfast when there's a loud knock on the door.

"Who could that be?" asks Mrs. Mitchell. She wipes her hands on a dish towel and hurries out of the kitchen.

When she returns several minutes later, Lily and Gene are with her. Lily won't look at us, and Gene looks very unhappy.

"Go ahead, Gene," says Mrs. Mitchell in a crisp voice. "Tell the girls what you told me."

"I heard a rumor," he says. "About a young soldier who is a spy and delivers coded messages on origami."

My eggs stick in my throat, and Nanea shifts in her chair.

"I happen to know the rumor is untrue," says Gene. "Do you know how I know?"

Nanea slowly shakes her head.

"Because Lily and I wrote those coded messages," says Gene.

Lily looks as sick as I suddenly feel. "We were just having fun," she says. "After our Nancy Drew mystery and watching the Sherlock Holmes movie, I thought you would know the notes were from me!"

"We didn't know," says Nanea, shaking her head. "Oh, poor Lieutenant Foster."

"What about him?" asks Mary Lou as she walks into the kitchen.

Mrs. Mitchell clears her throat. "Your sister just accused him of being a spy."

"What?" Mary Lou nearly drops the pineapple juice. "Nanea, how could you? He's serving our country. What if someone treated David that way?"

Nanea looks horrified at the thought. I am, too. *What if someone accused Dad of being a spy? What if he was arrested—for something he didn't do?*

"This isn't an imaginary adventure," says Mrs. Mitchell. "There's a real war going on. It's fought by real people, and there are real consequences for being careless with the truth."

Hot tears well in my eyes. If I look at Nanea right now, I'll cry for sure.

"You girls owe Lieutenant Foster an apology," Mrs. Mitchell says gently. "He's coming back for lunch today, so you'll have your chance."

Turn to page 159.

I know Mango's family misses him. But he trusts us—I can tell by the way he offers me his paw. And this curfew thing sounds pretty official. "It wouldn't be so bad to keep Mango for just one night, would it?" I ask.

Nanea doesn't think so. "Mele will be glad to have a doggie sleepover," she says with a smile.

So after a chicken dinner and a big slice of pineapple upside-down cake, Nanea and I settle into her bed with the two dogs. Mele must think it's too crowded, because she hops off to curl up on the floor. But Mango lies right between my feet, and pretty soon, he's snoring away. He's so cute!

"I know he's not mine," I whisper to Nanea. "But I sure wish he was. He makes me forget how much I miss my dad."

"Dogs are like that," she says. "I bring Mele to visit soldiers at the hospital. She reminds them of their own dogs at home and helps them forget their injuries for a while."

"Really?" I prop up on one elbow, trying not to disturb the dog at my feet.

"Sure! I call it Operation Mele Medicine because the

soldiers say she's better than medicine. You don't have to have a dog of your own. Sometimes you just need to borrow someone else's, even for a few minutes."

Like I did with Mango today, I think, settling back down. I wish I could have a dose of Mango Medicine every day. I fall asleep listening to his gentle breathing.

Turn to page 161.

"We're almost there!" Nanea says again.

We're walking to Tutu and Tutu Kane's house, which Nanea says is really close. But after hiking up Punchbowl this morning and practicing hula this afternoon, I'm tired!

When Tutu answers the door, she seems surprised to see us. She and Nanea put their arms on each others' shoulders and press their foreheads and noses together. Then they both take a deep breath. Afterward, Nanea turns her head so that Tutu can give her a kiss on the cheek.

"It's the traditional greeting," Tutu explains, embracing me in the same way. It makes me smile.

Nanea puts a record on and we perform our hula right there in the living room. As we dance, Nanea describes to her grandparents what we're seeing and doing.

Tutu watches me with kind eyes, and I try not to be nervous. *Dancing helps me feel less scared,* I remind myself.

"Very good," Tutu says when we're done. And then to me, she says, "Now you are beginning to know hula."

"I like it," I say. "It's fun!"

Tutu nods. "Nanea is a good teacher. To fall in love with hula is to fall in love with Hawaii."

I feel a lump form in my throat. "I never thought about it like that." How does Tutu know just how I feel?

I'll be leaving Nanea soon to go back to my family—I know it's time. But I don't want to leave her. And now I don't think I want to leave Oahu, either. What happened here, in just one day? My whole world turned upside down.

Turn to page 166.

Nanea and I are waiting in the living room when we hear the squeak of Lieutenant Foster's bike chain. She looks at me, and I look at her. When he comes inside, we apologize together, taking turns telling him what we did—and how sorry we are.

"It's all right," he says when we're done. "I'm glad it didn't get out of hand. You girls sure have big imaginations." He smiles when he says that last part.

Because he's being so nice, I ask him something that's still niggling me. "Lieutenant Foster, did you go somewhere last night? We heard you leave, and . . ."

"We were worried about you—because you went out after curfew!" adds Nanea.

Lieutenant Foster bursts out laughing. "So *that's* why you suspected me!" he says. "Well, that was my fault. I shouldn't have gone out. But sometimes, when my mind is full of worry, I can't sleep. It helps me to sit outside—to talk to the man in the moon."

"You were just out on the porch?" asks Nanea.

He nods. "Right outside the door."

Nanea apologizes again, and I do, too. But no matter how nice Lieutenant Foster is to us, I can't shake the feeling that we made a very big mistake.

When he follows Mrs. Mitchell into the kitchen, Nanea turns to me. "We really let our imaginations run wild, didn't we?"

I nod. "I wish we could have used them to *help* someone instead of hurt someone," I say sadly.

Nanea thinks about that for a while. I can almost see the wheels turning in her brain. Suddenly, she says, "I've got it! We can make *more* origami cranes and put them all around the neighborhood. Inside, we'll write messages in an easy-to-break secret code. The messages can tell people *not* to spread rumors!"

Nanea's idea sounds really creative. But it also sounds like a lot of work! After what happened with Lieutenant Foster, I'm feeling kind of homesick. And I'm missing Dad more than ever.

Is it time for me to go home? Or should I help Nanea with the project? I just don't know.

To tell Nanea that you have to go, turn to page 165.

To help with the origami project, turn to page 169.

We wake up to the sound of the doorbell.

"What time is it?" asks Nanea, stretching.

"I'm not sure, but it's time to let Mango out!" The dog is scratching at the bedroom door.

By the time we stumble out behind the dog, Mrs. Mitchell is in the living room with a woman and her little boy. "Niu!" shouts the boy, rushing across the room toward Mango.

Mango knows the boy, too. He practically knocks him down with doggie kisses.

"I'm sorry to come so early," says the woman. "Your neighbor, Mrs. Santos, said you might have our Niu. And you do! He ran away during the air-raid drill yesterday."

"Niu?" I ask.

"It means 'coconut,'" Nanea explains.

It's hard to think of Mango having a different name. And it's even harder to say good-bye. But I know it's time for him to go home to his family.

And it's almost time for me to go home to mine.

Turn to page 172.

Lily!" we say at the same time.

"Jinx!" says Nanea. "Wow, Lily really sent us on a wild goose chase. Let's go tell her we figured it out!"

As we run to Lily's house, I have an awful thought. "Nanea, what if we had accused Lieutenant Foster of being a spy?"

She shudders, as if the thought makes her feel cold. "That would have been bad. We could have gotten him into a lot of trouble. Good thing we didn't tell Mrs. Lin what we thought. She would have told *everybody.*"

"Good thing," I agree, remembering how I almost opened my mouth and let my suspicions spill out.

Lily is sweeping her front porch. When she sees us, her face breaks into a grin. "Well, it's about time!"

"That we cracked the code, you mean? But that didn't look like your handwriting! Your letters are usually so loopy," says Nanea.

"Gene helped me." Lily looks pretty proud to have thought of asking Gene for help. "He hid the secret messages. It made me feel like I was sleeping over with you two even though I couldn't!"

"But why did you put the notes by the soldier's bike?" I ask. "We almost thought that Lieutenant Foster was . . . oh, never mind." I don't even want to tell Lily what we thought. It's too awful.

"By the bike?" Lily wrinkles her forehead. "I told Gene to put them by Mele's water bowl. I knew you'd check that twice a day!"

"Oh!" Nanea shakes her head. "Mystery solved. That was pretty fun, Lily. You'll make a great cryptologist someday. It's an important job."

"And a tough one, too," I say. I'm a little embarrassed by how long it took us to read the messages.

I think back to our conversation about jobs for women. It was just yesterday afternoon, but it seems so long ago now!

We've helped a lot of soldiers since then, I realize, thinking of the bandages we rolled and the books and magazines we gathered. *And we avoided hurting a soldier, too, by stopping a rumor before it started.*

As we leave Lily's, I finally feel like I'm ready to go home—back to the beach and back to my family. Instead of reading about Nancy Drew all weekend, I had my own adventure with Nanea!

Will I ever be able to tell anyone about it? I wonder. Probably not. Who would believe me?

That's okay, I decide. *Maybe the best secrets are the ones we keep to ourselves.* I smile as I follow my new-found friend.

The End

To read this story another way and see how different choices lead to a different ending, turn back to page 70.

"I wish I could help you, Nanea. But I think it's time for me to go home. This whole thing with Lieutenant Foster makes me miss my dad," I say sadly.

I'm afraid she's going to be disappointed. But if she is, she doesn't show it. Instead, she sits beside me on the couch and says, "I feel the same way—not about Papa but about David."

"Do you think they ever have trouble sleeping, like Lieutenant Foster does?" I ask her. "I've been so busy missing Dad that I didn't think about how *he* feels, being away from us!"

Nanea has a faraway look in her eyes when she says, "Maybe some families are taking care of them, like Mom and Papa took in Lieutenant Foster."

"Maybe," I say. "I sure hope so. And I hope Lily can help you with your secret message idea."

Nanea brightens up. "She will, I think. Plus, she's better at origami than I am."

That gives me a bright idea of my own. "Before I go, do you think you and Lily could teach me how to fold a crane?"

Turn to page 171.

"I wish you didn't have to go," says Nanea. "I'm afraid we might not see you again. What if the government says you and your family have to leave soon?"

My two new friends are standing with me outside the Royal Hawaiian Hotel. This is where my family will pick me up, I tell them. And it's sort of true. But it's so hard to leave!

"Donna and her mom left the island so suddenly," adds Lily. "We barely had time to say good-bye."

"Having you here was like having a third kitten again," says Nanea. "I can't wait to write a letter to Donna and tell her all about you!"

"You and Donna would like each other," Lily adds. "You're both a lot of fun. You made hula really fun, too!" She smiles at me from beneath her shiny black bangs.

That gives me an idea. "How do you say good-bye in hula?" I ask Nanea.

"Aloha, of course," she says, waving her hand as she sways from side to side.

"How funny that one word means hello *and* good-bye," I say.

"And it means love," adds Nanea with a smile.

So my friends and I don't really say good-bye. We say aloha.

I wish I could write them letters, the way they write to Donna. *But there is one friend I can write to,* I remind myself. I'll write to Kayla as soon as I get home. *If the Three Kittens can stay in touch across the ocean, my best friend and I can, too.*

When Nanea and Lily are gone, I hurry behind the hotel and lift the puka shell necklace up and over my head. I'm ready to say aloha to my family again now.

I see my brothers right away, still building that sand castle. And then I see Auntie Oli. As I cross the sandy beach, I shade my eyes and look up at Diamond Head. The volcano is still there, too.

"It *does* look like a fish!" I say out loud, noticing how the high point of the volcano rises like a fin.

"Yes. Leahi." Auntie Oli calls to me. When she smiles, her eyes crinkle.

Mom was right, I realize now. Auntie Oli has done a lot to make us feel welcome here, just as Nanea and her family made me feel welcome. *Can I open my heart to Auntie Oli?* I wonder. I think I'm ready to try.

"Should we hike Leahi one day?" Auntie Oli asks.

"Yes!" I say, at the same time as my brothers do.

"Today!" says Aidan.

Auntie Oli chuckles. "Not today," she says. "But one day soon. We have time."

"We have lots of time," I say. I don't know where the words come from, but I know they're true. We may be here on Oahu for a while. And that's okay with me.

The End

To read this story another way and see how different choices lead to a different ending, turn back to page 15.

I decide that I have to help Nanea. I can't take back the rumor we spread, but maybe I can do something to make it *better.*

We get a notepad and make up a bunch of anti-rumor slogans, like "Cast rumors out to sea" and "Crack rumors like coconuts" and "Spread aloha—not rumors." Then we scramble up the letters and write the secret slogans on origami paper.

When Lily comes over, she shows me how to fold the paper into cranes, geckos, and *koi,* a kind of fish. Her hands fly so fast! Now I know why she was so good at rolling bandages.

"Ready?" asks Nanea when we're done. "Time to go out and hide them." Her eyes flash with excitement.

"What if we get caught?" asks Lily.

"If we do, it's okay," says Nanea. "We're not doing something wrong—we're doing something *right.* We're trying to stop rumors, remember?"

Lily smiles. "Right."

We each take a handful of the origami animals, and then we step outside. We tiptoe from yard to yard, as if we're on a big adventure.

Nanea tucks a crane in a flower bush. Lily hides a

gecko inside a wrapped-up hose. I tuck a koi inside an empty watering can. We place a couple of *extra* animals in Mrs. Lin's and Mrs. Santos's yards.

Wherever we go, we leave bright little reminders about doing the right thing. And it feels good.

Turn to page 173.

By the time Gene drops me off back at Waikiki Beach, I have my own origami crane. It's not perfect, but I know Dad will like it when I send it to him. Inside, I wrote a secret message. Dad will have fun unscrambling it, and when he does, he'll read this:

I miss you, but I'm doing okay. I hope you are too. When you miss me, just look up at the man in the moon. I'll be looking at him, too. I love you.

The End

To read this story another way and see how different choices lead to a different ending, turn back to page 160.

"Thank you for helping me bring Mango—I mean Niu—home," says Nanea, after the dog and his family are gone. We're sitting on the front porch, tracing lines in the red dirt with our bare toes.

"It was fun," I tell her. "And it felt really good to help Niu—to . . . what was the word Auntie Rose used for helping?"

"Kokua?"

"Yes, kokua. Helping Niu helped me feel better, too. And you were right—dogs are good medicine."

I reach out to scratch Mele behind the ear. I know I can't have a dog of my own. *But when I get home, can I borrow one somehow?* I wonder. Then an idea strikes: Maybe I have neighbors who have dogs that need walking! And maybe those dogs will lead to a few new friends—girls who love dogs as much as I do.

After all, it was a dog who led me to Nanea, I remember, leaning over to bump her shoulder with mine. *And friends are good medicine, too.*

The End

To read this story another way and see how different choices lead to a different ending, turn back to page 69.

By the end of the afternoon, I'm finally ready to go home. It's hard to say good-bye to my new friends, but Nanea gives me a sweet souvenir of our time together: a tiny pink crane.

After Gene drives me back to Waikiki Beach, I find the hole in the barbed-wire fence and step through. Then I reach for my puka shell necklace.

As I slide it off my head, I hold tight to that tiny crane, too. Will it still be there when I get back to my own time? I hope so! Maybe I'll use it as a bookmark in my Nancy Drew book—a reminder to use my imagination to *help* people whenever I can.

The End

To read this story another way and see how different choices lead to a different ending, turn back to page 133.

ABOUT Nanea's Time

In the summer of 1942, America had been fighting in World War Two for just six months. But for kids like Nanea, it was difficult to remember a time when the country *wasn't* at war. Everything changed when Pearl Harbor, the military base on Oahu, was bombed on December 7, 1941.

Unlike mainland America, Hawaii was a combat zone. Blackouts, curfews, and air raid drills were taken seriously. The military, and the people who lived on the islands, feared that there would be more attacks. Like Nanea, people tried not to be afraid, but there were constant reminders of war. Barbed wire lined the coast to keep enemy boats from coming ashore. Junker cars were parked in fields to prevent planes from landing in open spaces. Everyone had to carry a heavy mask at all times in case the enemy released poisonous gas into the air. And there were soldiers everywhere.

The increase in military personnel had a huge impact on all of Honolulu. More people meant long lines at stores, crowded buses, and a shortage of housing. It was also difficult to feed everyone. Almost all of Hawaii's food supply was shipped from the mainland. Once the war began, military supplies took up most of those shipments. To ease these shortages, thousands of women and children, like Nanea's friend Donna and her mom, had to leave.

The war separated families and cut off friendships, but it also created new ones. Many families opened their homes to servicemen stationed on the islands—just as

Nanea's family does with Lieutenant Foster. They welcomed strangers to boost the morale of the men who were fighting for America. Some soldiers and families kept in touch long after the war ended.

The war gave everyone new roles. Sons and brothers became soldiers. Children took on new responsibilities. Women stepped into jobs previously done only by men. The very first all-women's military organization began in Hawaii. The Women's Air Raid Defense group went into operation in January 1942. The WARDs worked in a top-secret location receiving coded messages that were used to track enemy aircraft. It was the first time in history that women directly contributed to the defense of American territory.

Children also took on new roles. There was a shortage of workers in the agricultural fields, so sugar and pineapple plantations hired kids. All during the war, boys and girls from grades eight to twelve spent one day a week working in the fields. Some students thought it would be fun to miss a day of school, but they soon found out how hard the work was.

When World War Two ended in 1945, women and girls had a new understanding about what they could do in the workforce and how they could contribute to their families and communities. The war changed the w[illegible] women viewed their roles, and that view has been evolving ever since.

GLOSSARY of Hawaiian Words

aloha *(ah-LO-hah)*—hello, good-bye, love, compassion

huli *(WHO-lee)*—a turning movement in hula

kaholo *(ka-HO-low)*—a side-to-side movement in hula

keiki *(KAY-kee)*—child

kokua *(KOH-KOO-ah)*—assistance, a good deed, to help

Leahi *(lay-AH-hee)*—Diamond Head Crater. The Hawaiian name means "brow of the tuna."

lei *(LAY)*—a wreath of flowers, feathers, or shells worn around the neck or head

mahina *(mah-HEE-nah)*—moon

mele *(MEH-leh)*—song

mu'umu'u *(MOO-ooh MOO-ooh)*—a long, loose-fitting dress without a train, usually made from brightly colored or patterned fabric

niu *(KNEE-ooh)*—coconut

'ohana *(oh-HAH-nah)*—family

poi *(POY)*—a starchy pudding made from pounded taro root. A *poi dog* is a mixed breed dog, named for a now-extinct breed that was fed poi.

puka *(POO-kah)*—hole. Puka shells have holes in the center.

taro *(TAIR-oh)*—a tropical plant with a starchy, edible root

tutu *(TOO-too)*—grandparent, usually grandmother

tutu kane *(TOO-too KAH-nay)*—grandfather

Read more of NANEA'S stories,

available from booksellers and at *americangirl.com*

Classics

Nanea's classic series in two volumes:

Volume 1:
Growing Up with Aloha
Nanea may be the youngest in her family, but she *knows* she's ready for more responsibility. When Japan attacks Pearl Harbor and America goes to war, Nanea is faced with grown-up chores and choices.

Volume 2:
Hula for the Home Front
The war has changed everything in Nanea's world. She's trying to do her part, but it's not easy to make so many sacrifices. Hula, and a surprising dance partner, help Nanea hold on to her aloha spirit.

Journey in Time

Travel back in time—and spend a few days with Nanea!

Prints in the Sand
Step into Nanea's world of Hawaii during World War Two. Learn how to dance a hula. Help a lost dog. Work in a Victory Garden, or send secret messages for the war effort. Choose your own path through this multiple-ending story.

A Sneak Peek at

Growing Up with Aloha

A Nanea Classic

Volume 1

Nanea's adventures begin in the first volume of her classic stories.

Sunlight slivered through the blinds. Nanea Mitchell stretched, breathing in the sweet outside smells of ginger and plumeria and the savory inside smells of breakfast. Sausage! Mele thumped her tail in anticipation.

"Good morning, you silly poi dog," Nanea said, giving Mele a pat. She hopped out of bed and turned the wall calendar from October to November 1941. It was Saturday, so Nanea put on a sleeveless blouse printed with tiki huts and palm trees and a pair of white shorts.

Her fifteen-year-old sister, Mary Lou, yawned, loosening her braids as she slid out of her bed across the room. She walked to the vanity, shaking her dark waves over her shoulders, and clicked on her little Admiral radio.

"Your hair looks nice," Nanea said.

Mary Lou picked up her hairbrush and turned to Nanea. "Let me fix yours."

"It's fine!" Nanea leaped out of reach.

"Alice Nanea Mitchell!" Mary Lou scolded, using Nanea's full name. Papa had picked Alice, which was Grandmom Mitchell's name, and Mom had picked

Nanea, which meant "delightful and pleasant."

"Sometimes you are so childish," Mary Lou sighed.

"Not today." Nanea picked up her *'eke hula,* a basket for carrying costumes and implements "See? I'm all ready for hula class."

While Mary Lou got dressed, Nanea made sure she had both sets of wooden dancing sticks. The *kala'au* were the size of a ruler; when she hit them together, they made a *tick-tick* sound like the big clock in her third-grade classroom. The longer *pu'ili* made a happy noise that reminded Nanea of the cash register at Pono's Market, her grandparents' store.

That reminded her of something else. "Why can't I go to work with you after class today?" Nanea asked. "Tutu says I'm a big help."

"Tutu spoils you," Mary Lou answered, fluffing her hair, "because you're the baby of the family."

Nanea knew that their grandmother did *not* spoil her, and that she was *not* a baby. But before she could say anything to Mary Lou, "Chattanooga Choo Choo" came on the radio. Mary Lou grabbed Nanea's hands and twirled her around the room, singing along with the radio.

When the song ended, Mary Lou said, "Gosh, that was fun." Her eyes sparkled.

"Hula is prettier." Nanea made the motion for swimming fish.

Tail wagging, Mele licked Nanea's hands.

Nanea laughed. "These aren't real fish, you goofy dog!"

"What's going on in here?" David asked as he ducked his head into the girls' bedroom, sending in a wave of Old Spice aftershave.

Nanea noticed the ukulele case in his hand. "You playing today?" she asked.

Seventeen-year-old David worked as a bellboy at the Royal Hawaiian Hotel, but sometimes he filled in when one of the other musicians was sick, or surfing.

"Maybe," he said. "I'm a Boy Scout. I'm always prepared." When her big brother smiled, Nanea thought he was as handsome as any movie star. "Breakfast is ready. Come on."

The girls followed him to the kitchen. "Good morning!" Nanea said, kissing Papa's cheek. His hair was wet from the shower.

"More like good night for me," Papa replied. He worked the graveyard shift, so he went to bed after breakfast, which was really his dinner. Papa was a welder at the Pearl Harbor shipyard. There were so many ships. And planes, too, at Hickam Air Field next to the shipyard. David said because Pearl Harbor was a big deal in the Pacific, Papa was a big deal in the Pacific. That always made Papa laugh.

Nanea turned to her mother. "Why can't I work at Pono's Market? I'm nearly ten."

Mom tucked a stray lock of hair behind Nanea's ear. "Don't be in such a hurry to grow up."

"Yeah, Monkey." David waved his fork. "Enjoy being a kid as long as you can."

"I would love to be nine again," Mary Lou said. "No responsibilities."

Nanea frowned. She had plenty of responsibilities! She took care of Mele and set the table and always turned in her homework on time. "Being the youngest doesn't mean I can't do grown-up things," Nanea said. She wondered why her 'ohana, her family, never gave her the chance to prove it.

About the Author

Like Nanea, ERIN FALLIGANT grew up reading Nancy Drew mysteries and dancing with her older sister to records on a record player. Unlike Nanea, Erin was lucky enough to grow up during a time of peace. World War Two was a distant memory, something she heard about in the stories her grandparents told. She's grateful for the sacrifices families like Nanea's made so that others could enjoy peace and freedom. From her home in Madison, Wisconsin, Erin has written more than 30 books for children, including advice books, picture books, and contemporary fiction.